WEIGHT FOR LOVE

JASON COLLINS

ACKNOWLEDGMENTS

A very special thank you to:

My cover designer, Cate Ashwood Designs.

My editor, Tanja Ongkiehong.

My proofreaders, Leonie Duncan and Shelley Chastagner.

Cover photographer Eric McKinney of 6:12 Photography.

CONTENTS

MARK

CLICK.

I pushed the key into the ignition again and turned it, listening in anticipation. Nothing. No chugging. No roar of the engine. Just that telltale click.

This was a sign. I just knew it. I was already conflicted about the idea of coming back to Winchester, the small town in South Carolina where I grew up, especially since I had gained weight, but this? It felt like a handwritten note from fate telling me in no uncertain terms that I had made a capital-M Mistake. This morning, when I'd first set out, I'd been in pretty high spirits. But I had driven all day to get here with nothing but my wandering fantasies of strong Southern men to keep me company, and as nice as the thought of rugged guys with tight, exposed abs was, every mile marker I passed gave me second thoughts.

I was doing this for my grandmother, so I could help her out while she was getting her home renovated. She had always been an exceedingly generous lady, and I worried her construction team might take advantage of that and give her an outrageous quote, if not something worse. Maybe that was a little pessimistic of me. But I loved my grandmother more than anyone else in the world, and I was protective of her. Besides, with my job as a freelance translator, I could technically do my work from anywhere that had Wi-Fi and an outlet for my laptop.

Taking a month-long stay in my hometown would be no big deal, right?

But now, just as I was pulling into a gas station within the city limits, my battery had evidently decided there was no better moment to tragically give up. It felt like the town was waiting for me to return so it could point and laugh at me one last time. Typical. I gave the ignition one more try, but to no avail. The battery was dead. I sighed and pulled out my phone, preparing to call my grandmother and ask for a jump start, when suddenly my attention was diverted by a big, black truck pulling up to the gas station. When I saw the man sitting behind the steering wheel, I nearly did a triple take.

And when he cut the engine and stepped out of the truck looking like a fine piece of sizzling sirloin, my jaw dropped. Dressed in form-fitting jeans, a flannel shirt half tucked in, and the kind of boots that indicated a man with outdoorsy interests, he immediately caught my eye. Especially when I realized that I recognized him, however faintly. The silhouette he cast reminded me of someone—a guy from my past. From many years ago.

Then it hit me.

That guy, the one with the broad shoulders, that sexy cowboy swagger, and the perfectly tousled hair was Carter Foster, an old schoolmate of mine a year ahead of me. He had always been gorgeous, even when we were both awkward teens, but now that we were entering our thirties? As much as I knew to keep my eyes off straight guys, Carter was beyond good looking. At least, he struck me as straight. Probably.

He was no longer cute in that scrappy country boy kind of way. He was tall and muscular and tough but put together. He looked as though he would be equally at home riding a horse through the mountain paths as he would sitting at a drafting table drawing up beautiful, precise blueprints for someone's dream home. I wondered if that was the path he'd taken. I could still remember him the way he was when we were in high school. He was a year ahead of me, but I often saw him in the campus courtyard, sketching away. Back then, Carter was too sporty for the art kids and too artsy for the jock kids, and yet he was an accepted member of both groups.

In fact, Carter was the kind of guy whom everybody liked. All the girls had crushes on him. All the teachers adored him. I had always nursed a little crush on him myself, even long before I came out as gay. Clearly, he had aged like a fine wine. Rather than being the adorable country boy I once admired from afar, he had transformed into a rugged, sexy Southern man. He was about as close to perfection as a man could be.

Even now, he seemed to glow under the bright sunshine of a clear spring day. I watched as he smoothly made his way across the parking lot, those athletic legs taking long, even strides. He jogged a little to reach the entrance so that he could hold the door open for a woman and a little girl. I could plainly see the words "you're welcome, ma'am" cross his perfect, sensual lips. It melted my heart to see him acting so courteously. It came naturally to him, I could tell. Growing up in the South would do that to a guy. Here was a man who you could depend on to revert to his sirs and ma'ams and please and thank you. The kind of guy who would sooner eat his hat than cause harm to anyone else. He was a true gentleman, and yet there was no doubt in my mind that he knew how to have one hell of a good time.

I wondered what it would feel like to fold myself against his muscular chest and rest my cheek on his steady heartbeat. Those big, strong arms alone would be enough to grab hold of me, clench me close, pin me up against the shiny black paint of his truck. I could almost feel his leg wedged between my thighs, the two of us rutting against each other while we each grappled for dominance, his lips pressing hard against mine. He had the ruddy cheeks and lean muscle of a man who often worked outdoors, and I couldn't help but imagine that he must be good with his hands. I pictured him strutting up to me, flashing that bright, infectious smile of his, making me go weak in the knees.

I was so caught up in my little mini-fantasy that it took me a good ten seconds to realize with a jolt that he had noticed me, too. And unless my eyes were playing tricks on me, he seemed to be looking at me the same way I looked at him. But that was impossible, right? Surely I wasn't even on his radar. But then he walked my way, his intense eyes fully focused on me. My heart began to race, and my hands were getting sweaty as I watched the man of my dreams come sauntering up to the side of my car, a roguish smile on his handsome face.

No. There was no way he could look at me the way I looked at him. That would be totally absurd. He was the very definition of masculine beauty, and I was...well, I was just Mark Sullivan. Former chubby high school kid, current chubby adult man. Nobody here in town knew about those years in between, that time during which I took good care of myself, when I became the version of Mark Sullivan I was most proud of. I was slick. I was slim. I was on top of things, finally pulling off all those big, lofty ambitions I used to daydream about back in high school when I was just watching the clock, waiting for math class to end.

Nobody knew about *that* Mark Sullivan. Especially not this Southern Adonis walking up to me like a fever dream come to life. I forced myself to smile and try to play it cool. *Just be normal, Mark. For once, don't embarrass yourself,* I thought.

"Good mornin'," the dreamboat said as I rolled down the driver's side window.

"Oh, hey. I didn't see you there," I lied.

He squinted at me, tilting his head to one side. "Pardon me, but you look awfully familiar. Do I know you from somewhere?" he asked, scratching at his chin.

I was so stunned by how hot he was I couldn't even summon up a single coherent thought to offer him. Luckily, he went right on talking.

"You're Mark, right?"

Realization crossed his face, and he grinned as he put two and two together.

"Mark Sullivan? I think we went to high school together," he said.

"Yep. That's me. And you're Carter Foster," I replied, blushing.

He chuckled, that gorgeous smile making me feel all warm and tingly inside.

"You got it. Good memory. Man is it wild to see you here! You moved off to some big city after graduation, didn't you?" he said.

"Uh-huh. I did. But um, I'm back now," I said.

Carter nodded for a moment, then went on. "So, you in town to stay, or just stoppin' by?"

Was that a note of hopefulness in his voice I detected? No. It couldn't be.

"Just stopping by. I mean, I'm staying for about a month, but not permanently," I clarified.

His eyes flitted to the key in the ignition, and he frowned slightly.

"What's goin' on there? Did your battery die or something?" he prompted, leaning in through the window a little. I could feel the heat rolling off his body in waves. I swallowed hard.

"What? Oh! Uh, no. Nope. It's totally fine," I said quickly. I pulled the key out of the ignition and laughed awkwardly. "I'm just here for some gas and a coffee. You know, fuel for my car and fuel for me."

I immediately regretted the stupid joke, but to my relief, Carter laughed.

"That's a good one, man," he said, patting the side of my car. "Well, it sure is nice to see you again, Mark. Enjoy your visit!"

"You too," I said, smiling, then immediately winced.

'You, too?' Really?

"Oh, hey. Let me move my truck so you can go first, huh?" he offered kindly.

Shit. I felt my blush deepen, my cheeks burning like crazy.

"You don't have to do that. I'm fine, really. Thank you, though," I said.

"Nah, it's no sweat off my back. I'm sure you've got lots of things to do now that you're back in town. Don't let me slow you down," Carter remarked cheerily.

As he turned to walk back to his truck to move it, I sighed and leaned out the window.

"Actually, Carter—" I called.

He glanced back at me, confused. I gestured for him to come back and he did, my heart hammering a mile a minute the whole time.

"What's up?" he asked.

He sounded slightly concerned, which was understandable considering how weirdly I was acting. What was wrong with me? What was it about this handsome man that got me so absent-minded and distracted?

"I guess I was wrong. Wouldn't you know, the battery *is* dead," I admitted.

Carter nodded slowly, then smiled. "Well, that's no problem! I'll get you jumped off in just a second, all right?" he suggested.

"That would be very helpful. Thank you," I said.

My face was burning as though I was standing on the surface of the damn sun. I had only been in town for less than twenty minutes, and already I was making a complete fool out of myself. What spell did this small town have over me? In the city, I was ambitious and successful. Put together. Clever. But here? It was straight back to the geeky, hapless nerd I was in high school. I was starting to wonder if I'd made a huge mistake by coming back.

I watched as Carter hopped into his truck, neatly turned it around to face the front of my car, and then hopped back out to pop the hood. He did the same to mine, giving me a thumbs-up.

"What do I do again?" I asked.

There was no use in trying to play it cool anymore. That ship had set out, sailed, and sunk already. Carter went to the back of his truck and pulled out some thick jumper cables, whistling cheerfully as he hooked them up between his truck and my car. He took the reins, guiding me through the simple but precise process of jump-starting my battery. People coming to the gas station gawked at us like it was the most exciting thing they'd seen all day. And when I remembered that this was, in fact, a small town, I realized that it might actually be the most exciting thing to happen here all week.

"Okay, now that these clamps are all on the right position, just give the engine a good rev of the gas," Carter instructed me. I bit my lip, worried that I would somehow mess this up.

I pressed on the gas pedal, and the engine chugged to life, but before I could smile with relief, something horrible happened. Carter let out a yelp and started shaking violently, like I had electrocuted him. My heart sank, and I jumped out of my car to run to him, but then I noticed that he was laughing.

"Sorry, man, just a little joke." He chuckled, grinning from ear to ear.

Relief washed over me, and I laughed. "Wow, you got me," I confessed.

I felt warm and fuzzy inside. I had grown up around these parts, and even though I'd been away for several years, I still knew that this kind of slapstick teasing was one of the primary ways a country guy like Carter knew how to show affection. It was like a secret language of sorts, one I had never been very fluent in when I lived here, but I could decipher it when I needed to.

"Couldn't resist," he replied. He gave me a wink and unhooked the jumper cables.

"Thank you for this. I'm glad you were around to save the day," I told him.

"Me, too. I'm always happy to be of service," he said warmly. "Anyway, I'll let you get back to your day. It's good to see you again, Mark. You look great, by the way. I hope you stick around for a while. In a town this small, I'm sure we'll run into each other again."

"I hope so," I said.

I offered my hand to shake, but to my surprise, Carter pulled me into a tight, albeit brief hug. My whole body seemed to light up from within, all the wires crossing in my head and my heart pumping like I was halfway through a marathon. In the two or three seconds we were pressed against one another, I marveled at the strength and control rippling through his body underneath his clothes. It was intoxicating, electrifying, like a sip of some potent illicit drug. I was burning, from head to toe. I felt like it was my body that had been given a jump start as well as my car. When we broke apart, Carter was grinning. He patted me hard on the shoulder, gave me a curt nod, and strode away back to his truck, leaving me standing there slack-jawed and tingly.

My thoughts were running in wild circles trying to make sense of the incredible stimuli I'd just experienced. On the one hand, I thought surely I was reading too much into the interaction. After all, Carter was just another handsome straight guy from the country, right? His kindness was courtesy, not anything more. But then... I could have sworn I felt something between us. Something hard. And it was not mine.

Just as I was forcing myself to dismiss that crazy assumption, Carter pulled by in his truck and paused to give me an almost sheepish wave goodbye. Maybe it was just a trick of my mind or the sunlight, but it looked like his cheeks were flushed a little. My heart skipped. As Carter drove off, something else dawned on me—he hadn't even filled his tank with gas. I smiled to myself, realizing he must have been so flustered by our serendipitous interaction that he flat out forgot to do what he came here to do.

But how could that be? In what universe would a guy like Carter be flummoxed by a guy like me? Sure, a lot had changed since high school, but back here in Winchester, none of that mattered. Everything here was exactly the way it had been all those years ago.

Wasn't it?

I shook myself out of my thoughts and filled up my gas tank. I pulled out of the gas station lot and back onto the main road, heading down the familiar side streets and quiet shortcuts to my grandmother's house. It was a route I could follow in my sleep, with my eyes closed. In a way, it was kind of comforting to know that no matter how many years had gone by, I could still so vividly remember the way back home.

As I drove along, I noticed all the familiar sights. I passed by the old school and shook my head, marveling at how much bigger and updated it looked. Back when I went to school there, the place had been pretty small. It was the only high school in town, and with a population so low, the school itself had been able to handle kindergarten up through twelfth grade all in one place. I had heard that a second school, an elementary academy up the road, had been opened in the years since I moved away. My old school was painted in black and green, our colors. There was a large sculpture of a buck standing proudly in front of the school, almost certainly handmade by a local artist. That was something our town was well known for: artistry. A good chunk of the adult workforce here revolved around sculpting, woodworking, painting, weaving—often with a focus on utilizing and highlighting local materials. It wasn't exactly a hippie town, but it was pretty damn close. People here were proud of where they came from, and most families in town had lived in the area for generation after generation.

Even though I had taken off for the big city after high school, I could understand why people would stick around Winchester. It was a beautiful place to grow up, between the dense, virgin forest land, the foothills of the Blue Ridge Mountains, the mist rolling down from the higher peaks, and of course, Lake Wren. The earth here was incredibly fertile and mineral-rich, with rough streaks of sparkling raw quartz studding many people's yards. The red clay dirt lent itself perfectly to sculpting. The plentiful flora was great for botanists and home apothecaries. There were so many different species of birds, insects, small mammals, frogs, deer, foxes, wolves, bears—it was a virtual menagerie. And then, of course, there was a nearly endless supply of strong, gorgeous lumber to be used for woodworking, which was probably the biggest artisanal export of the region.

I drove past the old bed-and-breakfast where my family used to live and work. To my delight, it appeared to still be in use, even though my parents had sold it and moved away years ago. They never minded Winchester, but they left once I'd moved to college, so my guess was they were just restless, judging by how much they traveled nowadays. It was nice to see the lights still on, the bed-and-breakfast illuminated with golden, rosy light. I could perfectly imagine all the different little lives intersecting in that house, people visiting to hike the trails or just enjoy Lake Wren or sample all the artisanal shops. I passed the same locally run grocery store my family used to visit on a weekly basis. It was still almost exactly as it was back then. The sign had been repainted out front, but other than that, it matched perfectly with the image I had of the place in my memory.

The sun was starting to set across the streaky blue and golden sky, the pink clouds fluffy and picturesque. I could feel the stress of the city rolling off my shoulders as I drove. A smile spread across my face, and my hands relaxed on the steering wheel. The tension loosened in my body. Everything seemed so peaceful, slowed down to half-tempo compared to the hustle and bustle of the city. Finally, the most welcome sight of all loomed ahead of me at the end of a long, quiet residential street: my grandmother's house.

I was home.

CARTER

WINCHESTER SEEMED BATHED IN A NEW LIGHT AS I DROVE AWAY FROM the grocery store, my mind still reeling from the detour down memory lane at the gas station where I had seen Mark Sullivan an hour earlier. I couldn't believe it. After all these years, he was back in town. I glanced in the mirror before taking a turn, and the first thing I saw was the faint tinge of color in my cheeks. I shifted in my seat, and I noticed the feeling of the tight denim pants brushing over the swollen outline of my shaft between my legs. I couldn't help but chuckle at myself.

My truck rolled over the smooth, recently repaved roads of the only town I had ever known, and I felt like I was in high school again for a few moments. I felt a powerful but subtle sense of freedom, the kind of freedom that reminded me of the days I could spread out a big blanket and stretch out next to someone feeling just as tense and free as me, happy to work out our energy with few inhibitions and fewer clothes. Over the years, my forearms had gotten thicker, and my hands had gotten a good bit rougher, but it sometimes felt like all those years had barely passed. I was a Southern guy through and through, and there was just something special about the smell of the morning country air on a long stretch of road when the sky was this clear and the sun was shining so bright.

It was days like these that reminded me why I loved it here so much. These pine trees and black gums, the cry of a hawk off in the distance, the occasional deer bounding across the roads, and the steady beat of small-town living—it was hard to beat if you asked me. Just as hard to beat as those country nights, where the din of crickets and the hooting of owls was all there was to hide the sounds coming from my bedroom when I had someone special to pin to my bed and spend the night with.

But a sleepy town like Winchester didn't get much news, and for us, a guy like Mark breezing back into town was definitely news enough to talk about. At least, it was news enough that I had forgotten to get the gas I stopped for at the station.

Had Mark noticed? No, probably not. Right? Why did it matter, anyway?

I shook the thought off and smiled at my absentmindedness.

When I came to a stop sign and brought my truck to a slow, silent stop, I shifted in my seat and realized I felt something hard against my thigh. My heart skipped a beat as I realized how stiff my shaft was, and then it took off fluttering again.

Well, Carter, maybe some things never do change.

Back in high school, Mark had always been someone I'd wished I'd had the chance to talk to more, but our social circles had never overlapped enough to give us the opportunity for that. At the time, I'd had no idea what it was that had first caught my eye about him, but he had been the kind of person I had always seen doing his own thing and wanted to get to know better.

It could have been any number of things about him. Every time I had crossed paths with the guy, he'd had a smile on his face, like nothing ever seemed to keep him down. He was human, of course, so I was sure I'd only seen that side of him like everyone else had, but the guy had seemed to let stress roll off him in a way I liked. And as cozy as those sweaters had looked, he'd worn them so well I hadn't been able to help but admire it. He had even had a nice laugh, and damn, it had been nice to hear that sound again.

I was getting ahead of myself, I knew. We barely knew each other back in high school, but even so, he was one of those guys who just stuck out in my mind. I hadn't been expecting those same old feelings to still be there, but it had only taken one conversation to remind me that they were most *definitely* still there. If anything, they'd just had time to grow.

Back in high school, I had no idea what they were. It just hadn't crossed my mind, and since Mark and I had never really run in the same friend groups, it had never been necessary for me to deal with them.

If I had, I might have realized back then that I had one king-sized crush on Mark Sullivan.

My love life back then had been just about like everyone else's, as far as I could tell. I'd gotten my share of dates, never had trouble getting someone to go to prom with me, and had known how to handle myself on anything from a quick hookup to a cozy dinner at the diner. Over the years, I'd had a few casual flings, but nothing serious. I'd mostly stayed focused on work. Still, I had never sat myself down and tried to come to terms with the fact that Mark was the only man I'd ever had a crush on, and apparently, still did.

Was that even something I had to come to terms with?

No, there was no need to overthink it, I decided as my truck turned the corner onto a rocky, unpaved road leading up to the mechanic I was headed to. I'd had plenty of time to realize that I had been into Mark, and that was as simple as that. It might have been a surprise that I still had that crush, but it was a nice one. There was no need to read into it more than that. I liked who I liked.

And now that Mark was back in town, maybe this was the chance to revisit those old feelings in ways I never could before. Or maybe I was getting ahead of myself again. I had a habit of doing that. Not that knowing so ever stopped me.

I brought my truck to a stop in an open parking spot at the shop, and the familiar sights and sounds greeted me. The old mechanic was well maintained, and you could tell how much love went into the place. It was early in the day, and the doors were open, but there was already a rusted old truck up high on a lift.

I knew it belonged to Sam before I saw the overall-clad old man talking to a cross-armed mechanic with a Southern accent so thick even we locals had trouble following along sometimes.

"Sam, I told you that you can't drive on these tires," the mechanic was saying, "much less take 'em on country roads like that."

"That's not even why I brought it in!" Sam protested, and the two went back and forth debating how drivable threadbare tires were while I watched my buddy Tyler emerge from the office and roll his eyes at the two with a smirk at me.

"What're you getting into today, Carter?" Tyler asked as he met me halfway across the gravelly parking area and gave my hand a firm shake with the usual grin on his face. "Don't tell me you're finally gonna let someone else touch your truck. I've got a bet going with Bernie."

"Not today, Tyler." I chuckled, giving his arm a pump before following him into the humble yet tidy office reception. "I'm looking to buy, but I don't know if you'd have to order what I need."

The smell of freshly brewed coffee met us as soon as we entered the office, and I drew in a deep breath that I let out with a smile as Tyler poured us a couple of cups. A rerun of the popular show *Bannister Heights* was playing on the office TV in the corner, with a grainy image of the infamous Adrian Bannister speaking dramatically to his latest starry-eyed fiancée.

"I swear, we're the only ones who genuinely like this crap," Tyler joked.

"The soap opera or the coffee?" I joked, because I knew for a fact it was the latter. "Someone's got to keep them in business." I elbowed him back. "Smell still takes me back to that summer I worked here with you after high school."

"Shit, you saved my ass that summer." Tyler chuckled. "My uncle's job offer is still on the table if you ever feel like moonlighting. So, what're you after?"

"Need a battery for a 2012 Chevy Malibu," I said.

Cars might have only been a hobby for me, but it only took a glance for me to know the make, model, and sometimes year of most vehicles. I credited most of that knowledge to having been friends with Tyler for so long. Tyler blinked in surprise, then furrowed his brow and looked me up and down.

"That's a fine car, but you never struck me as a sedan kind of man, Carter," he said.

"It's not for me." I laughed. "I'm just helping out a friend. Mark Sullivan just blew back into town."

"No kidding!" Tyler said, looking surprised and beaming. "Well, shit, where'd you find him?"

"At the gas station down the road with a dying car battery," I said. "Gave him a jump and sent him off, but I figured he could use a warmer welcome than that, so I'm getting him a replacement on me. I don't know how he feels about Winchester after running off to the city, but if he's going back, we ought to give him a good impression."

"I hear that," Tyler said. "I'll cover some of it too, give you a discount. I've got one that'll work just fine, in fact. Mark Sullivan, I'll be damned. Where's he staying?"

I opened my mouth to respond, but it occurred to me that I had no idea.

"Uh...now that you mention it, I don't think I got that from him," I admitted, scratching the side of my head.

"Get his number?" Tyler asked as he led me into the back, an area of pure organized chaos, a mess of parts and packages that only the employees could figure out.

"Mm, nope," I said.

"How long is he gonna be in town?" he asked, raising an eyebrow at me.

I gave him a look that told him I didn't know that either. Tyler was a good friend, but he didn't need to know that I had been way too distracted by flirting with Mark to ask any of that.

"Just gonna drive around Winchester until you run into him, then?" Tyler teased, grinning.

"All right now." I laughed, elbowing Tyler in the arm before taking a long drink of coffee. "I'll run it by his grandma's. If he's back in town, he'll swing by there at some point, I'm sure."

"Oh, yeah, he was really close with his grandma, wasn't he?" Tyler said, nodding. "Damn, you've got a sharp memory for that kind of thing."

I laughed, grateful that Tyler's back was turned to me as he looked through the shop for the battery in question so that he couldn't see the blush on my face until it faded. Finally, Tyler found what he was looking for, and he picked up a box to look over briefly before handing it over to me.

"Here's the one. Let's not worry about ringing it up. Just square up with me when you come in for coolant next. I know you're about due."

"And you say *I* got the good memory," I said.

"Got me there." Tyler chuckled. "But wow, Mark Sullivan wasn't a name I thought I'd hear again. Always thought he was an all right guy. I remember how Bill and Jarrod liked to run their mouths about him, but I don't think he really deserved that."

My smile faded a bit as I recalled what he was talking about. I had been an athletic guy in high school, which put me in the same social circles as the other athletes around my class. Some of them hadn't been the nicest people in the world, and while I had never been around to hear them saying it, I had always had a feeling that some of the guys I hung out with from time to time had probably said some unnecessary things about Mark, just like they had about a lot of people in school. They weren't anyone I could have considered close friends at any point, and I would have stood up for Mark if I'd heard them picking on him firsthand, but that was then. Bill and Jarrod were names I barely thought of anymore. That wasn't part of my life these days, and the more I picked up about how they'd acted back then, the happier I was for it.

"They really did that, didn't they? Jackasses. Well, I like to think if there's anyone who can give him a good impression on his homecoming, it's people like us."

"I hear that," Tyler said with a grateful grin. "So, heading back to the office?"

"Yep, got a few things to check in on before a meeting tomorrow morning," I said. "And got to make sure Dad's keeping his head above water."

"Take care of him, now," Tyler said.

"Always." I chuckled, taking the battery under my arm and nodding to him. "I appreciate it, man. I'll get back with you later."

"Sure thing. Don't sweat it!" Tyler assured me with a sharp nod. "You tell Mark I said hello, and tell him to get that ride in here if his big-city mechanic isn't treating him right, yeah?"

"Will do," I said, giving him a thumbs-up from behind as I headed out the door and back to my truck.

Tyler Pearson was good people. He had worked at his uncle's mechanic shop since about the time I started working at my dad's office, and I was proud to have him as a friend. We had been pretty close back in the day, and we were nowadays, too.

We were just guys who liked working with our hands, plain and simple. There was a kind of simple satisfaction I got out of taking a hands-on approach to everything I did, both in my job and in my professional life.

And it doesn't sound like a bad approach to my love life, either...

Thoughts of putting my hands on Mark drifted through my head as I drove. I wanted to slip a hand under one of his sweaters, feel his warmth close by me, see that smile cross his lips and that glint in his eye—

I shook my head lightly and ran my hand through my short hair, taking a deep breath and counting to ten as I made my cock settle down. I was going to have to get a handle on my body if I was going to make it through the day. I might have to do something about this once I had some privacy in my house tonight, though. Perks of living alone.

That thought certainly didn't help how excited my manhood was.

In short order, I pulled up in front of Foster Construction, the family business. No matter how many times I saw the sign—and I saw it daily—it made me happy to see. It was one of those businesses that had been in Winchester for over a generation, and if I had anything to say about it, it would stay that way. Dad was nearing retirement age, and as it was, I already took on most of the jobs that came through here, like the one I'd be handling first thing tomorrow morning.

I had always been a hands-on kind of guy. It should have been no surprise that I had become a general contractor like my father and his father before him. Better yet, it gave me the chance to see Winchester grow and change slowly firsthand. Being able to build your own hometown was a kind of joy that was hard to find anywhere else.

But as I climbed out of my truck and headed up to the office door, I couldn't keep away that feeling that always snuck up on me: it wasn't quite as nice as it could be with someone to share it with.

And just like that, once again, my thoughts drifted back to Mark.

MARK

MY ANXIETY ABOUT RETURNING TO WINCHESTER WAS ALREADY FADING.

Of course, running into Carter and seeing how friendly and happy he was to see me certainly helped. The whole drive from the city to Winchester, I had been trying to fight off the feeling that I was walking blindfolded into a pit of snakes. Perhaps that was a little dramatic, though. After all, it wasn't like the town of Winchester itself was so inhospitable to me.

I actually had a plethora of warm memories of growing up here, running around barefoot in the woods, getting covered with sticky pine sap, crunchy leaves, and red clay mud. I had never been an especially athletic child, mostly because I disliked the feeling of having a full team of other players depending on me, but that didn't mean I spent my entire adolescence hiding away indoors. I used to go fishing with my neighborhood friends on the silty banks of Lake Wren. We rarely caught anything besides tiny minnows and frogs that clung to our fishing lines, but it was less about hooking something impressive and more about just enjoying the scenery and the peace. I used to play make believe in the foggy, green woods, creating these elaborate dreamscapes in my mind. I could be an intrepid explorer, blazing new trails through an untouched wilderness. I could be a mystical wizard on the search for some magic gem that would give me the power of flight or invisibility. I would climb trees and hop across the smooth, flat boulders peeking out of the creek water. I would hit the library, find some cheesy 70s fantasy novel, tuck it under my arm along with a bottle of juice and a snack, and head out into the woods, hunting for the perfect spot to curl up and read.

It was a different time back then, before it was less common to turn kids loose on the world to roam all day. Back then, my parents trusted that within the city limits of Winchester, there was little in the way of harm that could come to me. And in that regard, I imagined Winchester had probably stayed the same. I couldn't remember the last time a violent crime had been committed here, if it had ever happened in the first place.

Of course, there was the occasional petty theft or graffitied bridge in the forest, but for the most part, crime was nonexistent. There was enough for everyone to go around. Neighbors were all too happy to share, and if anyone found themselves between a rock and a hard place, there was always someone else willing to pick up the slack. People here were quiet, slow-moving, and content. For the kind of people who would flock to an artsy, sleepy small town in the Carolina countryside, this was about as close to heaven on earth as one could get. Nobody wanted to dispel that magic. Everybody here worked together to keep Winchester magical. To keep it safe. I could see why people stayed here even after high school graduation was long past. Some people were totally satisfied to just stay here, continue the family tradition. This was the perfect place to raise a kid, and there was always enough work for everybody.

When I had first left Winchester for college, I had convinced myself that I was moving up the ladder, that I was doing something better and more impressive than the folks back home. But over time, I was beginning to acknowledge that happiness came in a different package for every individual and that for a lot of people, Winchester was the perfect package.

It didn't take me long to get across town and roll into the long driveway in front of my grandmother's house. My heart swelled with warmth as I took in the familiar scenery. To the left of the driveway rose the old blueberry bushes, reaching so high that they were almost more like trees. Their branches were speckled with berries in shades of dusty blue, lilac, and green. To the right were the shiny holly bushes boasting tight red berries. Bees hummed and buzzed around the brush in their endless hunt for pollen. The yard stretched on for many yards off to either side of the house, filled with trees and bushes and flowers.

Grandma Nancy, even though she was in her seventies, was still very active and self-motivated. She was always a little obsessive about her yard and garden, and it was a relief to see everything still so well maintained. That indicated to me that she was still mobile and capable of taking care of it all. I was certain that the clean mountain air and easy pace of life was part of what kept her so healthy and happy well into her golden years. People here lived a long time. It was kind of a running joke around town that there had to be something in the water because Winchester was known – among other things – for the longevity of its residents. It was almost as though the land nourished those who nourished it, and my grandmother certainly fit into that category. She could make even the most finicky, frail plant bloom and flourish under her care and attention. Throughout my childhood, everything I ever learned about gardening and the natural world came from Grandma Nancy. My science teachers had nothing on her. They tried, and they did a great job, of course, but nobody could make an afternoon of mushroom-hunting more exciting and enjoyable than my grandmother.

As I pulled up the drive, a rush of nostalgia and warm memories came hurtling through me. I couldn't stop smiling. The house in front of me, tall and broad with a wraparound porch and gorgeous old bones, seemed to almost glow from within. I looked up at the second-story bay window and sighed happily. It was the window to my old bedroom, the place where I spent so much of my childhood and teen years cooped up in the cold winters reading, playing video games, making up lush fantasy worlds in my imagination.

I lived with my parents at the bed-and-breakfast they ran here in town, but I spent a lot of weekends and off time with my grand-mother. Whenever the bed-and-breakfast felt overly busy and cram-packed with strangers, I would retreat to my grandmother's house for some peace and privacy. She was always happy to see me, always offering me delicious home-cooked comfort food. If I needed to be alone for a while, she would let me. If I wanted someone to talk to, she was there. Growing up, this house was a refuge for me. A safe place.

Our family spent holidays in Grandma Nancy's house, gathered around the gigantic Christmas tree in the den or feasting on local produce and meat in the dining room, perfectly cooked by my grand-mother and mom. This place echoed with warmth and joy. Every window I looked to reminded me of another stay, another day of peace or playtime. My grandmother used to play board games with me or watch movies with me in the living room. We would pick wild-flowers and press them between the yellowed pages of old books she'd found at estate sales. There were so many golden afternoons spent lazing around, just enjoying each other's company. Grandma Nancy had always "got" me, even when my friends and parents seemed to misunderstand me. Those rosy feelings still existed for me today. I couldn't wait to see Grandma Nancy again. After the years of hard work and nonstop go-go-go of my life in the city, I needed a respite, and she was always there to offer it.

I turned off the engine, making a mental note to figure out a way to buy a new battery for my car and get it installed soon, and then I made my way up to the front porch. I set my one old suitcase against the wall and rang the doorbell, rolling back and forth on the balls of my feet much like I'd done as a teenager coming to visit. My heart fluttered as I heard my grandmother's voice call out something across the house, then the telltale thump of her slippers on the wooden floorboards. I was grinning even before she reached the door.

She opened the door and immediately let out a gasp of joy, throwing her arms around me in a big hug. I laughed and gently hugged her back, the tension whooshing out of my body at her familiar scent. She had been using the same lavender perfume ever since I was a child, and the smell of lavender was still a soothing smell for me all these years later.

"Oh, my sweet grandson!" she gushed, pushing back to gaze up into my face.

"It's so good to see you," I said with a smile.

She reached up and patted my cheek, her crystal-blue eyes twinkling with emotion. The lines in her face had deepened slightly, and there was something a little more delicate about her now. That was to be expected. She was older now, and she needed to take things more slowly. But her eyes were the same, always as bright and clever and affectionate as I remembered them.

"Come on in, sweetheart. I am so glad to have you home," she chirped.

"I'm happy to *be* home," I murmured softly.

"How was your drive? Was the traffic okay? I heard on the radio there was an accident up near Durham, and I got a little worried it might delay you a little bit," she chattered happily as she trundled down the hall.

She had her long silvery hair tied back into a messy, artsy braid down her back, and she wore a vintage apron around her waist. She had always been a fan of thrift shopping, and Grandma Nancy still boasted an impressive closet of vintage clothing. She would buy old, worn-out pieces cheap from the secondhand stores and then take to her sewing machine, expertly stitching and re-hemming and needling new life into them. I was happy to see she was still up to those old tricks. She was the kind of woman who always needed to have a project going on, which was probably why she was so excited about the renovations.

"No, traffic was all right. Nothing worse than the usual bumper-to-bumper stuff near the research triangle. I'm used to it by now," I told her.

"Oh good. I always forget what it must be like to have all those cars crowding the streets. I don't think I've got the patience for it, myself!" She chuckled.

I followed her, carrying my suitcase down the hall to the dining room off the kitchen. I looked around, taking in all the little details that still remained, as well as noting some of the differences. The house was, after all, going through renovations. Although I adored this house, I could begrudgingly admit that it needed some TLC. It was an old house, and while I knew my grandmother would never let them alter the original charm of the place, we as a family had decided it was time to make some improvements. There were some safety concerns, too, and with Grandma Nancy getting older, it was important to make sure her home was safe for her to live in alone like this. She was fiercely independent, but everyone had their limits. One of the reasons I had felt so compelled to come visit was to make certain all those safety measures were properly installed. Grandma Nancy was likely to overlook them since she was so confident in her abilities to keep herself safe.

"I do hope you've got an appetite, my love," she said brightly. "I've got a roast in the oven, and I'm planning on a big country supper to welcome you back to Winchester."

"For your cooking, I always have an appetite," I told her.

She beamed at me. "Wonderful. Oh, it's so good to see you. I'm just delighted. Come along, Mark, let's get you settled in your old bedroom. I hope you don't mind I've spruced up the place a little bit. But don't worry, I left up all your old posters and whatnot," she assured me.

I laughed. "It's okay. It's your house, Grandma. You can change whatever you like."

She made her way up the broad, glossy wooden staircase with me following close behind.

"I know, but it's nice to keep your room sort of like it used to be. Don't tell anyone, but sometimes I peek in there from time to time just to look at it. So many nice memories of you coming to stay with me for the weekends. Do you remember?" she mused wistfully.

"Of course, I remember. It wasn't that long ago," I reminded her gently.

She nodded, her eyes sparkling. "Right, right. The times all sort of blend together once you get to my age." She laughed it off.

"Your age? You're barely fifty years old," I teased.

She looked positively tickled by the underestimate. "Oh, you flatter me, dear. Come on now, set down your suitcase. I'll give you a little time to get settled in and cleaned up, but then you'd better come on down for supper. I've invited your old friend Hunter over for the meal, too. I hope you don't mind," Grandma Nancy said.

"Really? That's fine. It'll be nice to see him again," I said with a smile.

"Okay, love. I'll leave you to it," she said with a smile, then shuffled off back downstairs to the kitchen to make dinner.

I glanced over at the vintage alarm clock on the nightstand by my old bed. I chuckled to myself when I saw that it was barely past six in the evening. Typical. My grandmother had always been an early diner. But then again, she had been getting up at the crack of dawn to start on her gardening for as long as I could recall. I looked around my old room and sighed, feeling both weary and content at the same time. Grandma Nancy was right – she had preserved most of my bedroom as it was back in the day. My old car posters were on the wall. There was my ancient, secondhand guitar leaning in a corner, and even though my old sci-fi bed sheets had been replaced with a more neutral plaid patterned set, there was still a cylindrical robot figurine perched on the window sill. In another corner there was the unfortunate scorch mark on the wooden floor where I had dropped a match trying to light a candle when a storm blew out the power one weekend in my sophomore year of high school. This room, just like the rest of the property, positively thrummed with sepia-toned memories. I smiled and shrugged off my coat, then walked into the en suite bathroom to splash some water on my face before heading back downstairs.

I got to the kitchen just in time for Hunter to come walking in with a broad smile on his face. He looked almost the same as he did back in the day except for the bluish five-o'clock shadow along his jaw.

"Mark!" he exclaimed.

"Hey, man! How's it going?" I greeted him. We shook hands while Grandma Nancy looked at us happily.

"Oh, it's lovely to have you boys back in the house. And you're just in time to set the table, too!" she gushed, gesturing to the glistening stack of fancy plates, bowls, and utensils on the counter.

"Ain't that typical. We've been in the house for five minutes, and she's already puttin' us to work," Hunter joked.

Grandma Nancy laughed delightedly. "You want to eat, right?"

"Yes, ma'am. Especially if you're cookin'," he replied graciously.

"Then get to work!" she chirped playfully.

Hunter and I did as we were told, and within ten minutes, we were all seated around the big dining table with a veritable feast of southern comfort foods among us. There was roast chicken, buttery mashed potatoes, homemade cornbread, and black-eyed-peas cooked in bacon grease. We sipped beer and loaded up our plates, chatting and catching up on the years gone by.

"So, Miss Nancy, what all do you have these boys doin' on the house?" Hunter asked.

"Well, mostly they're just fixin' up some of the places where the walls are showin' through, things like that. They're helpin' me replace some of the windows that cracked from that hard freeze we got this past winter. And then they're redoin' the guest bathroom down the hallway since the tiles are getting kind of grimy. This place has great bones, but she needs a little pick-me-up," she explained.

"Don't we all." Hunter chuckled.

"Mhm. That's right. I told the contractor, I said, 'now don't you go changin' everything around, mister, because I like my house the way it is' but I think he gets it. He's a good boy. Really knows his stuff," she said.

"What's the guy's name again? Carl? Wait. No." Hunter paused. "Carter. That's it."

I dropped my fork with a clatter, and they both looked at me.

"Goodness. Are you all right?" Grandma Nancy asked, eyes wide.

"Yeah. Yeah, I'm fine. But, Hunter...did you say the contractor's name is Carter?" I pressed him.

Hunter nodded slowly.

"Uh-huh. You remember, right? We all went to school together," he clarified.

My heart began to pound. I leaned back in my chair, a million thoughts ricocheting around in my mind. What were the odds?

"So, you're telling me the contractor in charge of fixing up the house is…" I trailed off.

Grandma Nancy beamed. "Carter Foster, mhm. He's doing a great job, too."

CARTER

"Heading over to the Sullivan house now?"

I looked up at the sound of my father's voice as he stepped into my office with his usual gruff smile and a box of doughnuts in hand. I smiled at him as he set it on my desk and opened it. I wasted no time snatching the maple one out of the assorted dozen like I always did.

"Yes, sir," I said before holding the pastry between my teeth while I finished packing up the papers I was sorting through. "Just need her to sign off on a few things before we get the work underway, make sure she has everything she wants exactly how she wants it. Think this might be the one renovation that isn't turning a historic house into a B&B, so I'm excited to hit the ground running on this one."

"Glad to hear it," Dad said. "Hope you don't mind, I looked over the paperwork last night just to look over your shoulder."

"I'm not about to get chewed out, am I?" I asked with a boyish grin up at him after ripping off a chunk of doughnut and nearly swallowing it whole.

I could eat like a wolf in the morning, but I burned through so much throughout the day that it never seemed to show. Mom always told me I just kept a teenager's metabolism.

"Hell no!" Dad laughed. "On the contrary, I was going to say I like what I see sketched up so far. You've done some fine work here, son."

I felt my heart swell with pride at that, but I did my best not to let it show. I could accept a compliment for hard work, but I had never let myself get arrogant, and I wasn't about to start.

"Well, thanks." I chuckled. "I wouldn't let a house like this one have anything less than the best."

"I'm sure Miss Nancy appreciates it, too," he said with a nod. "She still tells me how much she loves that shed you built for her son back when you were first starting out."

"That was a good shed," I admitted wistfully.

Most jobs came and left my mind as soon as they were done, but good work stuck with me. The job I was about to start was one I'd like to think of that way. For good measure, I put a couple extra dough-nuts in a small brown paper bag for later.

"That reminds me. How's that pet project of yours coming along?" he asked, walking with me toward the door. I got my folder under my arm and held my keys in one hand and my travel coffee mug in the other, doughnut bag perched on the lid.

"It's getting there," I said with a grin, not wanting to give away too much. "Don't go spreading the word just yet. I don't want to hype it up before it's finished."

"Don't know how you find the time for that thing, but if there's anyone who can pull something like that off, it's you," Dad said.

He had picked up a habit of reviewing the projects I was working on and commenting on them more than usual, I had noticed. Dad was in good health for his age, like most older people in Winchester, but I didn't have to be a detective to pick up on the hints that he was looking at retirement in a few more years. He was just making sure that the company was in good hands when he left it. I never felt like he didn't trust me. He just liked reminding me that he was keeping an eye on things, and I didn't mind that in the least.

"Take it easy, Dad," I said as I carefully got my precarious stack of goods into my truck. "And good luck with the hospital job. I'll bring lunch by the office around noon!" I added as we waved to each other before I pulled off.

I was practically glowing today. I had two things to look forward to: working on one of the houses I admired most in the town and running the very welcome risk of encountering Mark again. That had stuck with me in the back of my mind all afternoon yesterday, from the time I went back to work to the time I got home.

And that was why it couldn't have been more of a welcome surprise when I drove down the winding road to the old Sullivan house and saw a familiar sedan parked in the driveway. My face brightened, and I suddenly felt caught completely off-guard before I even stopped the truck and climbed out.

The house was something to behold, in my opinion, even in the state it was in. It was two stories tall, with chipping beige paint and a light gray roof that had survived all the hurricanes that made it this far north. The bay windows on the east side of the house on both stories had always drawn my eye every time I drove past it, and whenever I saw the woods behind it, I imagined what kinds of things we could do with that space if Miss Nancy ever wanted to try taming it. Her beloved garden was one thing, but with a house like this, there was always so much more potential just around the corner.

Folder under my arm and food in hand, I climbed out of the truck and knocked on the front door, heart pounding. It nearly popped out of my chest when the door swung open and it wasn't Miss Nancy, but Mark who stood in the doorway.

He looked surprised, but then a smile appeared on his face, and that made my mood soar.

"Well hey, stranger!" I greeted him. "Didn't think I'd see you again so soon. Make it home okay yesterday?"

"Hey! Yeah, absolutely," Mark said, a little flustered. "Thanks again for that. You really did me a solid. But I think I'll need more than a jump in the long term, so I might swing by the shop later with my grandmother's car. She's in the bathroom, by the way, should be out in just a few. You should have told me you were the one working on the house. I would have had you over last night with me and Hunter."

"To tell you the truth, I was so surprised to see you again it slipped my mind," I admitted with a chuckle. "But hey, on that note, let me save you a trip. Follow me back to the truck. I've got something for you."

I felt Mark's eyes on me as we crossed the yard back to the curb, and I had to admit the thought that he might be checking me out excited me, even if I was just imagining it. It had been a long time since I had been this worked up, and it was everything I could do to keep from showing it. Maybe it was something about the springtime air.

At the truck, I set everything on the roof and took out the battery to hold up to Mark, whose eyes widened in surprise.

"Oh wow, you're kidding!" he said, grinning in appreciation.

"Consider it a welcome home present," I said, trying to make it clear in my tone that this was no big deal, even though his gratitude was making my day. "Tyler says hello, too. We take care of our own here in Winchester."

"Well, thanks, Carter, you didn't have to do that," he said, blushing.

"No, but Tyler has a 'no returns' policy, so don't try going back to pay him," I said with a wink.

Before Mark could reply, Miss Nancy emerged from the door and waved to us. I waved back, and we approached the steps again while Mark set the car battery down by the door.

"Hey, Miss Nancy," I greeted her. "Ready to get this show on the road?"

"Carter, you know I'm just about ready to start swinging hammers on my own," she said, and Mark and I exchanged a quick grin.

"I just have a few papers here for you to sign before we can do that," I said, following her inside with Mark and taking out my folder. "Liability waivers, since you're going to be staying upstairs while we do the work, and a few more odds and ends to confirm that you're ordering the work done and understand all the technical stuff I went over with you last week. Everywhere you need to sign is highlighted, and I can explain anything that doesn't make sense."

"Leave that with me. I'll get it squared away," Miss Nancy said, taking the papers from me and nodding. "Don't you worry. You've already broken it down more than enough for me, sweetheart. Why don't you show Mark around and let him know what all you're going to be working on?"

Miss Nancy, wingman of the year!

"I guess I could do that," I said, grinning over at Mark, whose eyes had gone wide for a moment. "What do you say, Mark? I've got a little breakfast for us if you're hungry."

I held up the bag of doughnuts as proof, and to my surprise, Mark looked hesitant for a moment. I could have sworn I saw his eyes flit up and down my figure, and he scratched the back of his neck, chuckling.

"I already ate, but I suppose it couldn't hurt. I'm usually not awake until later, so my body is telling me it's time to eat again already."

"Well, I got the best ones from the dozen my dad brought to the office today, so best we not let 'em go to waste if you want an excuse," I said playfully as I handed him a chocolate cake doughnut.

Miss Nancy disappeared into the kitchen after waving us off again, so I nodded for Mark to follow me as I led him through the house. I dug through my folder to take out some of the plans I had sketched up as we headed toward the front door.

"So, what are you doing these days that has you waking up after eight thirty?" I asked.

"To be fair, I don't *have* to wake up this late," Mark said. "My schedule is whatever I want it to be, which is why it's a little bit of a mess sometimes. I'm a freelance translator."

"Get out of here!" I said, genuinely impressed. "That's wild, man. So, you work from home?"

"I can work anywhere I have a Wi-Fi connection," he said. "Setting your own schedule is a double-edged sword, though. I love my job, but if I don't stick to a schedule, it keeps me up at odd hours. Which means I'm almost always up at odd hours."

"I hear that." I laughed, thinking back to my little secret project I probably spent too much time on. "I'd be right there with you if language were my strong suit. I've always been more of a hands-on kind of guy. Though when you think about it, translating is always hands-on, isn't it?"

"I don't think I've heard that one before, but I'll take it." Mark laughed after a bite of the doughnut. "Wow, I missed the doughnuts here. These from that place off Main Street and 4th?"

"You know it," I said proudly. "I don't go as often as I used to, but sometimes I cave and pick some up if I've got a long day of hard work on the job ahead of me."

"I know that feeling," Mark said. "My job tends to have me in a café already, though."

"So the first thing I want to do here," I said as we got out to the yard, and I turned around to walk backward as I spoke, "is get a wrap-around porch for the whole house."

"Oh, that's perfect," Mark said, his face lighting up. "My grand-mother has been talking about that for years. There were a few times that she was just about to cave and order the work, and I always got excited at the idea of running around a full porch on those summer nights when they'd set us loose to play."

"Isn't it a good house for it?" I agreed, grinning. "Here, take a look."

I set my sketch on the hood of his car and then beckoned him to look at it. In the sunlight, we had to crowd close to get our shadows to cover it and keep the glare out of our eyes. Immediately, I felt his hip bump mine, and my heart fluttered, but I didn't call attention to it. I could feel his heat radiating on me, though, and that was hard to ignore.

"Right here is the golden spot, on the west side, because she'll have the shade from that gum tree to keep the sun out of her eyes while the sun sets," I explained.

"Wait, is all this your sketch?" Mark said, looking over the draw-ing. "I know it's your job, but wow, these are good."

I grinned, taken aback, but before I could stop myself, I bumped his hip in response, giving a light chuckle. My face went pink, and so did Mark's, but even though he swiped his tongue over his lips, he didn't acknowledge it.

"It's nothin'," I said modestly. "Your grandma painted a clear picture of what she wants. See here. This is the kitchen, which she's really going to gut. That's the part we're putting the most work into. I don't know how she'll survive without cooking for a while."

"What's this over here?" he asked, pointing to something in the yard.

"Oh, that's over here," I said, leading Mark over to a spot on the east side of the house. "All this land here, she wants to use to dig out a small pond for fish, and I'm building a small bridge for her to walk over."

"Oh, that sounds so peaceful," Mark gushed, looking around the area with an expression on his face that told me he could picture it perfectly. "She could come out early in the morning with some food for the fish…"

"…sweet tea in hand while she watches the sunrise, nothing but the birdsong in the air and the sound of fish troubling the water under the bridge," I went on with a broad smile on my face, envisioning Mark and I doing that exact thing.

"Sure you aren't moonlighting as a poet?" Mark asked playfully, raising an eyebrow.

"I swear, I double as an interior designer sometimes." I chuckled, and it was my turn to rub the back of my neck. "Or exterior, in this case."

"Sounds like the house is in good hands," he said warmly.

"Don't you worry. I'm not about to let a place like this get the wrong treatment," I assured him. "But besides that, I'm going to repair the creaky stairs and replace the banister, and she might have already mentioned the guest bathroom and the en suite she wants to add to the master bedroom. We're also going to touch up the roof and repaint the whole place a pale blue that is going to really pop in this shady patch."

"You put a lot of thought into your work," Mark pointed out, putting his hands on his hips and smiling at me.

"Sounds like we have that in common," I said without missing a beat, flashing him a grin, and there was that blush again.

A pause came between us, and we were suddenly all too aware of the tension hanging in the air. Here we were, two guys who really hadn't had enough of a relationship with each other back in the day to be so friendly right now.

Now or never, Carter. You know what to do.

"So, are you gonna be here for the whole time the renovations are happening?" I asked, tucking the papers back under my arm.

"Yeah, actually," Mark said. "I don't know. I just thought Grandma Nancy could use some company while the house is a mess. My parents have been keeping busy since they moved away, but my job lets me go wherever, so I thought it would be a good time for a visit."

"Then why don't you swing by my place for dinner tonight?" I offered. "We can catch up on how Winchester has been changing since you left. And I want to hear more about this translating job of yours," I added.

"Um—sure! That sounds great," Mark said without missing a beat, brightening up immediately. "Should I bring anything?"

"Just you," I said, realizing only too late that it could be taken a different way.

Not the wrong way, though, I couldn't help but think.

"I couldn't show up empty-handed." He chuckled. "Do you like wine?"

"A red would be perfect," I said, nodding.

"Sounds like a plan," Mark said brightly, even though the word *date* was on the tip of my tongue.

Before I could say more, Miss Nancy appeared at the window, waving at us. We exchanged a glance, laughed, and Mark led me inside to finish the paperwork.

My heart was racing a mile a minute. It really shouldn't have been. I wasn't about to get ahead of myself that fast. This was just dinner, after all. Totally not a date.

Totally.

MARK

I WALKED QUICKLY ACROSS THE PARKING LOT BEHIND THE GROCERY store, pulling my scarf more snugly around my neck and shoulders. I had a bottle of red wine tucked under my arm, hastily selected after probably at least twenty minutes of standing in the wine aisle, paralyzed with indecision. I had never been a very big wine drinker, and back in the city, I was often stuck at home writing into the wee hours of the morning, usually with a hot toddy or a screwdriver or something. Not wine.

Therefore, I was not especially well versed in the world of wine drinking and had no idea what a good choice off the shelf was. I had ended up deciding on a cabernet sauvignon with supposed cherry and vanilla notes, and I would be lying if I didn't admit that a large part of my decision-making process relied on marketing. I picked the one with the most attractive shiny golden label, hoping that good branding would translate to good taste. I just hoped Carter wouldn't catch on to the fact that I was a sucker for good marketing. I slid into my car and turned the key in the ignition, the resulting rumble of the engine reminding me once again of Carter's generosity in gifting me a new car battery. I blushed to myself just thinking about it. Car batteries weren't exactly cheap. He had done me an enormous favor. I only hoped I could find a way to repay him properly for it.

Of course, I could think of a few ways to pay him back...but I had a feeling it wasn't the kind of repayment plan a guy like Carter would be interested in. After all, he had to be straight, right? I could clearly remember him the way he used to be in high school. Lanky, strong, tough, athletic, popular – a typical country boy who dated country girls and grew up to raise country families. And yet, there had been something slightly off about the way he invited me over for dinner tonight. There was something more. I wasn't optimistic enough to assume it was some kind of thinly veiled date situation, but I couldn't deny that there was a little voice in the back of my mind begging the question: *was* this meant to be a date?

"Nope. Don't even go there," I told myself aloud as I pulled into the driveway in front of Carter's place. "It's just a catch-up session between acquaintances. No big deal."

As I rolled down the driveway, I found myself intrigued by the house itself. It was an unusual build for the neighborhood, and I could clearly see signs that Carter had customized bits and pieces here and there. That made me smile. I had always been entranced by other people's passions and seeing someone take such pride and genuine enjoyment in his work was truly impressive to me. There were so many people in this world who hated their jobs, who just rushed through life flitting from one boring dead end to the next. But I could tell Carter truly liked his work and found ways to incorporate his skills and his passions into his daily life. Plus, there was the fact that he was quite simply good at it.

The house was very charming, much smaller than my grandmother's place, but certainly not lacking in character. It was perched neatly on a hill, the backyard sloping rather steeply down into the piney woods below. Beautiful leaves of gold, orange, and garnet lay scattered all around the front yard, perfectly complementing the wooden paneling of the house itself. It was relatively compact and an unusual shape, with hints of DIY projects you could notice if you paid close enough attention. I could see there was a garden of sorts built carefully along the back slope of the yard, a sort of terraced style I recognized as being popular in the Italian countryside. And off to the other side of the house, I saw an obviously handmade structure made of wood and wire – a large chicken coop. When I turned off my car and the engine quieted, I could hear the chickens softly squawking and chirping to one another. I had always liked birds, and it warmed my heart to imagine a guy like Carter lovingly doting on the chickens in their coop. I was willing to bet he was the kind of pet owner who spoiled them rotten. Hanging between two thick oak trees in the front yard was a hammock, perfectly placed to get the most sun. I pictured Carter stretched out in the hammock, his brow furrowed as he lost himself in the pages of a book. It was an adorable image in my mind.

I parked and walked across the yard to the front door, noticing the chickens getting all riled up and excited at the sight of me. They all fluttered and rushed to the side of the coop closest to me like they were clamoring for my attention. That warmed my heart, too. I knew chickens were naturally very skittish, so for them to be excited rather than terrified of a newcomer indicated to me that Carter must spend a lot of time with them. I raised my fist and knocked at the door, clutching the bottle of wine while my heart thumped hard.

A few moments later, I heard the shuffle of footsteps, and the door creaked open. Carter was grinning at me, a faint blush spreading across his cheeks. I held up the wine.

"I brought this," I said a little awkwardly.

"Perfect," Carter replied. "Come on in!"

"Thank you," I said, following him into the house.

I noticed immediately that it smelled cozy and warm, the aromas of southern home cooking wafting through the house from the kitchen. I breathed in deeply.

"Wow, I don't know what you're making, but it smells heavenly," I remarked.

"Why, thank you. It's kind of a twist on stuff my mom used to make when I was a kid. Don't get me wrong, I love good old-fashioned southern cooking, but now that I'm a grown-up with my own kitchen, I try to modify the recipes to be a little more, uh, health-conscious, I guess you could say." Carter chuckled. "All the comfort but with a little less lard, you know?"

"I definitely get that. I love my grandmother's cooking, but sometimes it feels like I'm just shoveling butter into my mouth." I laughed. "I'd be lying if I said I didn't kind of miss it, though. Can't get real down-home food in the big city."

"No, you certainly can't. But I'm sure you'll get your fill of it while you're in town," he replied with a bright smile. "So let me give you the quick and dirty tour of the place, yeah?"

"Sure. Sounds great," I replied, trying not to fixate on Carter's perfect lips forming the words *quick and dirty*. He led me through the house from room to room, noting all the specific little alterations and personal touches he'd put on the place. It was obvious that he poured a lot of blood, sweat, and tears into making his home reflect who he was as a person. I found that trait to be exceedingly attractive. Carter was a man who knew exactly what he wanted and let no obstacles stand in the way of getting what he wanted. As someone who was usually too exhausted and tangled up with my busy work schedule to put much thought into my living space, I found Carter's house impressive. No one could ever accuse Carter of not caring enough – he seemed to throw himself headlong into every little project he took on. Meanwhile, I had been putting off my dream of backpacking in South America seemingly my entire adult life. It was inspiring to see someone who reached out and grabbed whatever he wanted out of this existence. Maybe I could learn something from being around a guy like him.

"Your house is amazing, Carter," I told him. "I can really see how you've put your own spin on things. I don't know how you do it. Back home, I kind of accept things the way they are. I never think too deeply about changing it up and making it my own, you know?"

"Well, thank you," he replied with a shrug. "But I see my house as an extension of myself. Everything here is designed to make my place more comfortable and open to guests like friends and family. I just want people to feel at home here."

"You certainly have accomplished that," I told him.

He beamed with pride. "That's good to hear. So, what's your house like in the city?"

I snorted. "Well, it's not a house at all for starters. It's a cramped little high-rise apartment. Just big enough for me to stretch out and get comfortable while I'm writing. It's all right. It's got all the basic requirements for a comfy landing pad. But it's not like this. Not by a long shot," I admitted.

I felt a little self-conscious comparing this homey, cozy house in the woods to my utilitarian, minimalist studio apartment in the city. My place seemed a little soulless by contrast.

"I guess it's true what they say: location, location, location," Carter said. "I bet your place is right smack dab in the thick of it, right?"

I smiled. "Yeah. It's centrally located in the city."

"See? And that's what matters for city living, isn't it?" he pointed out, making me feel infinitely better about my choices.

"You make a fair point," I agreed. "Damn, that food smells good. What are you making? Can I help with anything?"

"I think I've got it all under control," he said. "Unless you're itching to help me whip up this lemon-caper sauce I've got on the menu for tonight."

I lit up instantly. "Oh, of course! I'd love to jump in and help cook. Truth be told, I tend to live on a lot of takeout back home in the city. I live alone, and it's hard to justify taking the time and effort to cook for myself these days," I confessed.

"I get that. It's hard to cook for one person. Most recipes are created with a whole damn family of four in mind, seems like." He chuckled. "But I've found that cooking for myself makes me feel better at the end of a long day. It may look like a lot of effort, but it usually pays off, in my opinion."

"That makes sense," I agreed.

Carter worked on the pan-fried chicken legs and brussels sprouts while I whisked together a buttery lemon-caper sauce on the stove beside him, taking instruction from the master whenever necessary. I was impressed with how at ease he was in the kitchen, and I wondered if there was anything at all Carter wasn't good at. After all, he could build and design anything, he knew how to jump-start a car battery, and now he was turning out to be some kind of modest Michelin-starred chef. I couldn't help but feel magnetically drawn to him. He was like a bright, shining ball of light in the world. It was intoxicating just standing next to him over the stove, his side occasionally brushing up against mine as we cooked together.

Finally, dinner was ready, and we set the table together. It was amazing to me how easily and naturally we fell into a routine, both of us seemingly in tune with the other. He served up the crispy, fragrant legs of chicken along with the slightly charred, flavorful brussels sprouts over which I drizzled the lemon-caper sauce. When we sat down at the table, my mouth was already watering from the delicious smell. Everything looked expertly cooked and seasoned, more like a five-star menu than a home-cooked dinner. The lemony sauce dripped and collected in the crisped edges and layers of the sprouts, mingling with the salty broth from the juicy chicken legs.

I hummed my appreciation as I took the first bite. "Damn," I murmured. "This is seriously fantastic, Carter. Where did you get this recipe?"

He thought about it for a moment, then shrugged. "You know, I don't even remember. I think I might've made it up, to be honest." He laughed.

"Well, then, if you ever get bored of contractor work, you could definitely make it in the culinary world. I'm serious. This is amazing," I gushed.

"You're too kind," he said bashfully.

"Where did you learn to cook like this?" I asked.

"My mother, mostly. But I've always had a knack for cooking, if I do say so myself. Truth be told, though, I think it's a natural part of living in the country. Fewer restaurants, but fresher produce and meats and whatnot. I can't exactly drive down the road to some fancy restaurant whenever I so please, so instead I just learn how to cook whatever it is I'm craving," he explained.

"I forget about that sometimes," I mused. "Living in the city, I have just about any kind of cuisine you could think of readily available, but it's a double-edged sword because it's more difficult to justify cooking for myself. Although, for a while there, I was doing an okay job of coming up with healthy meal plans for the week. I even started working out on a daily basis. Nothing crazy, just a little cardio to get my blood pumping. But then winter came around, and it was too cold to go jogging around the neighborhood – or at least that's the excuse I fed myself."

"It's hard to keep up a routine like that, especially when you're busy," Carter said.

"But I mean, if you can do it with the kind of intensive work you do, I sure as hell ought to be able to keep it up." I sighed.

"Nah, it's different for everyone. You can't compare yourself to others like that," he said gently. "You have such a cool, interesting job. You live in a cool, interesting city. That makes you a cool, interesting person, Mark."

I was taken aback by how wise and compassionate his words were.

"That… that's one of the most comforting things anyone has said to me in a long time, you know that?" I said.

Carter smiled. "Well, then maybe you ought to hang out with guys like me more often."

"So, anyway," I pressed on, "how's work? And how have things changed around here since I moved away?"

"Honestly, you know how it is. Winchester is slow to change. It's like this place has a big bubble around it, cushioning it from the outside world. Things are good here. I guess people don't really see any big reason to change it," he noted. "But what about you? I bet your job is really exciting."

"Sometimes," I relented. "A little bit. Translating work is a lot of long hours in front of a computer screen, but I really enjoy it. I haven't done as much traveling as I'd like to, but translation work sometimes feels like taking a mini-trip to another country, if that makes sense at all. Plus, I like taking someone's idea and transforming it into something that makes sense to a broader audience. Helping people spread their ideas and connect with the world is really rewarding. Definitely makes up for the all-nighters."

"Damn. I could never do that. An all-nighter? I'd be wrecked for days. If I don't stick to my usual sleep schedule, I just fall apart," Carter said.

"I guess I'm just used to it at this point," I replied. "Though sometimes I do think I'd probably be better off if I could get my sleep schedule more regulated."

We kept talking throughout dinner, catching up on the years since we went to the same high school together, and when we were finished eating, we headed out onto the back porch to sip wine and watch the sun set. Just as I feared, the conversation inevitably turned to high school.

"You and I ran in different circles back then, huh?" Carter pointed out.

"Yeah. We did," I agreed. I took a big sip of my wine.

"I remember you, though. You were always so nice and friendly," he said.

I blushed. "I used to think you were so cool. I mean, I still do," I admitted.

Carter chuckled softly. "It's kind of a shame we weren't closer back then. Some of the guys I ran with... well, they weren't the nicest boys around," he said.

"Nobody likes who they were in high school, I don't think," I declared.

"Amen to that," he responded. "But I gotta say... I like who I am now. And I know you just got back, and we have a lot of catching up to do, but I like the person you are today, too."

I looked over at him and was nearly bowled over by the look of pure affection and honesty on his handsome face. Warmth spread throughout my whole body, and I felt something shifting between us, the tone of the evening morphing from casual hang out to...something more. Something stronger. Undeniable and unignorable.

I shivered a little in the evening breeze, goose bumps popping up on my skin. Carter seemed to notice this.

"Hey, man, would you... you like to come back inside? It's gettin' a little chilly out here, huh?" he said slyly.

I nodded fervently. "Yes. Yeah. Good idea."

We hurriedly got up and went back inside, both of us downing the rest of our wine as the tension mounted ever higher between us. It was apparent now – it wasn't all just in my head. There was some kind of electrical magnetism between us, something powerful that threatened to take control. We stood in the kitchen, at opposite ends of the counter, just staring at one another. Then, without a single word, Carter set down his wine glass with a clink and walked toward me. My heart pounded so hard I could feel it in my ears. Was this really happening?

Carter closed the space between us in a few short strides and cupped my face in his warm, large hands. He gazed into my eyes for a brief, intense moment, and then he dove forward, pressing his lips against mine. I moaned softly and melted into his arms, letting go of all self-control as he pinned me to the counter. His lips moved sensually against mine, our bodies rocking gently together from side to side, almost like a dance.

The heat sparked between us brighter and hotter until finally we were wrapped up in each other's arms, tangled together as we fumbled down the hallway to his bedroom, unable to keep our hands off of one another. We fell into bed under the low light of the sunset through the windowpane. Carter kissed me harder, his hands roving hungrily up and down my body while I rocked against him. I could feel his cock stiffening hard against my thigh, and my mouth salivated for a taste. When I broke our kiss, I could hardly move fast enough to get what I wanted. Carter was on his back, braced up on his elbows with his chest heaving and his gorgeous eyes heavily lidded.

I moved down the bed and positioned myself between his legs, tugging his jeans and boxers down. His massive, swollen cock bounced free in the crisp air, and I wrapped both hands around his shaft, pumping up and down slowly at first, then faster and harder. Carter closed his eyes and tilted his head back, groaning as I knelt to pull the engorged head of his shaft between my lips. He tasted warm and slightly salty, and pure adrenaline coursed through my veins as I eagerly sucked him off. He was panting now, his hand trailing down to press softly at the back of my head. He was desperate for me, for release, and I was equally desperate to give it to him. This was not the time for slow, thoughtful lovemaking – it was a time for fast, hard pleasure. I bobbed up and down on his cock, moaning and humming while he stiffened and throbbed in my mouth.

"Oh, fuck," Carter murmured, rolling his hips to meet me.

I sucked him harder and faster, determined to taste him.

"Just like that, Mark, oh god," he groaned, the breath catching in his lungs.

He froze up and gasped, his cock spurting thick, salty come down my throat. I swallowed it down eagerly, pumping his shaft through the waves of incredible pleasure. Carter all but collapsed, his chest rising and falling heavily as I licked my lips and flopped down beside him in the bed. He yanked the sheets up over us, the two of us tangled up in sticky bliss, our heads spinning with wine and exhilaration. It didn't take long before he drifted off, snoring softly beside me. The events of the past couple days seemed to catch up to me all at once, and I fell asleep comfortably nestled in Carter's strong arms.

CARTER

THERE WERE SOME MORNINGS YOU JUST *REMEMBERED*, ONES THAT YOU couldn't explain but that captured that feeling of safe, restful peace in the faint morning light like nothing else in the world could. That was what I felt when I woke up next to Mark the next morning. I opened my eyes to see his form still in bed right at dawn, sleeping like a rock. The sheets were halfway up his face, which left only his closed eyes, nose, and hair exposed as he slumbered. The direct morning light hadn't reached him yet. It was only still the palest blue outside, so I had a little time before the sun woke him up if I could keep quiet.

I slid out of bed as carefully as my bulky frame could manage, and I stood up to realize how stiff I was already. I gave my cock a quick stroke, feeling a little leftover tension from last night roll off me sweetly as I looked down at Mark. I wasn't about to explore myself while he was sleeping, obviously, but I couldn't help but admire the way he looked in the morning glow. But I couldn't just stand there and watch his chest rising and falling gently.

I wanted to do something special for Mark.

After a quick detour to the bathroom, I pulled a black bathrobe over my shoulders and tied it at the waist as I headed down the hall and toward the kitchen. It was another clear day, which told me I'd have to act quickly if I wanted to beat the sun to what I had in mind. I slid the glass door to the back porch open and headed outside, feeling the cold wood under my feet as I headed down to my garden.

I was always up at this time of the day, regardless of whether I wanted to make a guest feel welcome. The feeling of the garden first thing in the morning was an almost sacred feeling, like you were in a space that nothing could intrude on, all to yourself. I didn't understand how people could live without one. Even when work was at its most stressful, there was little that some quality time with the plants out back couldn't at least help.

The sound of the chickens clucking in their coop greeted me as I descended the couple of steps to the soft earth. I made my way over to make sure a fox hadn't gotten to them overnight, but I was happy to see that my design continued to prove fox-proof for the time being. The chickens were pretty self-sustaining, as far as livestock went. With nothing but some PVC, a simple motor, and some wood, I had rigged up a system that automatically opened the coop door for the chickens every day at dawn and closed it every night at dusk. The chickens had long since learned to head in on their own, but I still went outside most nights to make sure they were all accounted for.

And indeed, all the familiar feathered faces were out and about, scratching at the dirt. I took out some seed and fed them quickly, then headed over to the garden to grab a pair of scissors and get what I came out to get. I had to slip on a pair of gloves for this part, but it would be worth the effort.

I knelt beside the controversial addition to my garden in the far corner: stinging nettle. I collected a few handfuls of the soft stems with stinging leaves, then went to harvest some chives as well. I needed eggs for what I had in mind, but thankfully, the chickens had already given me such a backlog of eggs that I had resorted to giving them away to anyone who would take them.

I headed inside with my haul just as the morning birdsong started up in earnest, and I was deviously pleased to find that Mark hadn't gotten up while I was out there. I still had time.

The first step was to make the nettles safe. I put them into a pot on the stovetop and bit my lip at the sound of the clicking gas stove before the blue flame appeared. After adding a little salt and water, I pushed the nettle leaves around until they went limp, releasing their juices. They were entirely edible after rinsing them in a strainer, so I was free to chop them along with the chives without gloves. I then got out the milk, sharp cheddar, and homemade butter, and I was ready to cook the best damn six-egg omelet I knew how to make.

It wasn't long before I was listening to the sweet sizzle of the beaten-egg mixture in the pan that filled the kitchen with the rich smells of herbs and egg. Just a few minutes after that, I heard the sound of someone stirring in my bedroom, and my heart beat faster as I realized Mark must have been up and active. That was my cue to start the coffee machine.

The aroma of rich, dark roast coffee had filled the kitchen by the time I heard the soft creaking of the wood and heavy footsteps coming my way. I smiled up at the hallway just in time to see a groggy-looking Mark emerge and yawn, covering his mouth quickly and blushing in mild embarrassment.

"Morning," he said cheerfully, beaming at me as he approached the kitchen and blinked around at everything in surprise. "Your bed is unbelievably comfy. What's all this?"

"Thanks." I chuckled. "The bed frame came from one of the woodworkers in town, believe it or not."

"Oh, I believe it," Mark said. "The wood has that kind of rich smell you only get in the wood around here. ...not that I sniffed the bed frame," he said quickly, and I burst out laughing, shaking my head.

"Hey, man, no judgment," I teased, approaching him and planting a kiss on his cheek. "That's the first thing I did when I got it. Anyway, 'all this' is breakfast," I said, gesturing to the kitchen with a proud smile on my face.

"Wow, you know how to wake up a guy in the morning," Mark said with an uneasy chuckle. "It smells incredible."

Mark followed me over to the omelet in progress. I already had a couple of plates set out with some freshly cut fruit and a dollop of yogurt on each, more for garnish than anything else. The sizzling pan drew the eye most, though. The edges of the disk of egg were just starting to crisp up enough to tell me that the bottom was perfect and ready to be flipped. In the moist center of the mixture, the cheddar cheese was melting and bubbling softly with the buttery milk and textured nettle leaves, and the chives were sitting in a bowl on the side, ready to be added to the top of the omelet.

I couldn't deny feeling a hint of pride at how wide Mark's eyes were at the sight of the food cooking before us. I slid my spatula under it and flipped it over into a recognizably omelet shape, and the runoff egg and cheese hissed in the metal pan together.

"Wow," was all Mark could muster. "Is that spinach?"

"Nettle, actually," I said. "I know what you're thinking, but no, it's totally safe once you cook it down the right way, and I've had plenty of time to practice. I hear it makes a mean tea, too, but I haven't tried to make any yet. Oh, shoot, I forgot to ask. You can handle dairy, right?"

"Oh, yes." He chuckled. "Carter, this all looks incredible."

"Thanks, man," I said, feeling a little heat in my cheeks. "I dunno. I just thought you'd like a little something homegrown to start the day off. Call it my way of showing appreciation," I added with a wink that made his smile grow so much he had to look away. "Hey, you like coffee?"

"Definitely," he said, and while the omelet sizzled, I quickly poured us some coffee in two thick mugs shaped like pots of honey with handles.

"Milk is on the counter there, but I've got some creamer in the fridge," I said.

Mark went to the fridge and opened it, looking at the creamer thoughtfully for a few moments, then seemed to change his mind and go for the milk instead. He leaned against the counter and blew on his coffee as the rich dark brown gave way to a creamier mocha color, and he peered at the breakfast that I was finishing up. I used the spatula to cut the omelet in half and put both servings on two plates and sprinkled the chives on top.

"Carter, this is all amazing," Mark said after a few moments. "I appreciate it."

I turned to him, leaned in, and kissed him on the cheek, smiling.

"I appreciated last night," I shot back. "And it's pretty sweet what you're doing for your grandma, so I think you deserve to get spoiled a little."

"Hah, that's what she seems to think, too," he said, then shook his head a little. "But yeah, last night was…incredible, honestly. I had no idea you—I mean, are you?"

"Am I what?" I asked, blinking as I held up the two plates full of food and nodded for Mark to sit at the kitchen table.

Mark hesitated for a moment before saying, "What I'm getting at is, how do you feel about last night? Us, I mean? I remember you in high school, and you seemed pretty happy with the kind of people you dated back then."

"Ohhh," I said as it dawned on me at last, and I nodded slowly as we sat down together. "I gotcha. Yeah, I can see why that would be confusing." I attacked my omelet and chewed on the first bite thoughtfully for a few moments, thinking it over before speaking again. "To tell you the truth, I never gave labels much thought, y'know? You have feelings for who you have feelings for. That was me back in high school, and that didn't change a bit. All I know is I feel like a million bucks about last night, to tell you the truth," I admitted with a grin. "And unless you don't feel that way, I don't see why I need to try to read into it more than that. You know what I mean?"

"Yeah, yeah, totally," Mark said, looking more relieved than I might have ever seen him and smiling more openly. "I feel great about last night too. I just wanted to make sure you were on the same page."

"Well, consider breakfast my way of telling you I am." I chuckled, holding up my mug of coffee, and Mark raised his to mine to clink them together.

"I'll drink to that," he said, and we did.

We took a break to put a dent in breakfast, and I was happy to see how ravenously Mark ate. I didn't consider myself much of a chef. I was happy to cook when I had guests over, but I usually didn't get fancy like this. Mark just brought out something in me that made me want to impress. I liked seeing him take pleasure in what I could do with my hands, in every way, it seemed.

"This is insanely good," he said when there was only a third of the omelet left, dabbing his mouth with a napkin. "And this is all from your garden, you said?"

"Eggs from the chickens, herbs from the garden," I said, nodding. "I can only take half credit for the butter, though. I got the milk from a friend and made it out of that, and everything else came from the store."

"I had no idea healthy food could taste so good," Mark said.

"Well, I don't know if you could eat much more of a portion than this and still call it healthy. It does have a good bit of cheese in it," I admitted.

"Still fresher than anything I've been eating the past few years." Mark chuckled. "I've got to admit, coming back home has reminded me that takeout every other night with a job at a computer probably isn't doing my body too many favors."

"Your body seems plenty capable to me," I said, surprised to even hear myself saying the words.

"I—" Mark started to say, but my flirting took him by surprise, and he blushed as I grinned over at him and winked. "Well, back at you, if that's how you want to play," he teased.

"Maybe it is," I shot back, feeling my cock stir between my legs.

"I guess what I mean is that it's refreshing being back in Winchester," Mark said thoughtfully, "and it's got me thinking. Maybe I need to do some 'catching up' to run with it like I used to, if that makes sense."

"I'm not sure I follow," I said, furrowing my brow and taking a drink of black coffee.

"I know I probably don't look like it now," he said, twirling the fork around in his fingers, "but I actually slimmed down a *lot* right after I'd graduated high school and moved away. College was where I really spread my wings, I guess you could say. I was at the gym a lot, always swimming, running, all that kind of thing.

The only 'freshman fifteen' I got was the weight I lost, not gained."

"Whatever makes you feel good, that's the important part," I said, nodding. "And hey, I don't care what those assholes back in high school said to you. You look great. You always have and still do."

"I appreciate it." He chuckled, and I felt his leg brush against mine affectionately under the table. "But it's not so much a thing about looks as much as lifestyle. I don't exactly *love* feeling like I've let my life get out of shape."

"I mean, a successful translator living on his own in the big city who still knows his roots enough to come back home to help his grandma out doesn't exactly sound 'out of shape' to me," I pointed out, leaning forward and smiling matter-of-factly.

"Man, I'm never gonna get through this incredible breakfast if you keep making me blush like this." Mark laughed, and I joined him, reaching across the table and taking his hand in mine. It was soft and strong at the same time, and I brushed my rough thumb over the top of it for a moment.

"So, what do you have in mind?" I asked, worried that he was going to suggest something silly like a fad diet.

It made me feel a little sad that Mark was anxious about his weight. I had never given it a second thought, neither back in high school nor now that we were literally in bed together. He was an independent and confident guy who I found ridiculously attractive regardless of his size, but I wanted him to be happy, so I wasn't about to shut down his line of thinking, either.

"There's a gym in town, right?" he asked, tilting his head. "Like, the kind with personal trainers and that kind of thing?"

"Yeah, actually, I don't know if you remember Mason Glass from high school, but he's the trainer there. Has been for a few years now."

"I think I might head down there today," he said, looking up at me as if he liked that idea. "I mean, I'll be here for about a month, so it might be worthwhile to put my spare time to good use."

"Only if you feel like that's something you want to do," I said, nodding. "I've got your back, whatever feels right. Just don't get so wrapped up in all that that it keeps you away from me too long," I added with a wink.

"I wouldn't dream of it." Mark laughed, and he squeezed my hand back, smiling sweetly at me. "And hey, I appreciate the support. That means a lot to me."

"Of course, man!" I said, standing up to take our plates and kissing him on the cheek before carrying them to the counter to clean up. I looked over my shoulder at him. "Besides, if you're going to be looking for cardio anyway, I know a few ways to make that happen."

Mark had to turn his head again to keep me from seeing how much he was blushing, and I chuckled as I looked back to my dishes and got to work.

Damn, it was good to have Mark back in town.

MARK

I STILL COULDN'T WRAP MY MIND AROUND THE FACT THAT I HAD SPENT last night in another man's bed. And not just any man – a golden guy like Carter. As I slid behind the wheel of my car in his driveway, my heart was still thumping so hard it almost ached. My body was still ringing with the memory of Carter's muscles and sinew moving against mine. Every single place he'd touched still thrummed with a sort of magical echo. I could hardly wait to get in front of a mirror and find all the places he had touched me. I even hoped I would find some bruising, some red marks where he'd pressed too hard in his fervor or kissed too hard with passion. I wanted all those spots to glow and stay on my body as reminders of the amazing night we spent together. I could still so vividly taste his come beaded on my tongue, feel the silky smoothness of his cock sliding in and out of my mouth. My bulge twitched a little with renewed desire as I turned the key in the ignition and felt the engine rumble to life. Just thinking about the way Carter's beautiful eyes closed slowly and his lips fell open in a desperate sigh was enough to get my engine revving again. He was gorgeous. He was magic. And I was hooked.

But I couldn't quite shake that insecure little voice in the back of my head that clanged like a bell to disturb the good vibrations of the morning after. It kept warning me that it was a fluke, a one-off event that would never happen again. Maybe the stars had just aligned for that one evening. Maybe it was the red wine. Maybe it was the way the sun-streaked golden and pink across the sky, setting the world in a rosy, sensual glow. Maybe it was just a moment of weakness, a lapse in judgment on his part, if not mine. But then, he hadn't seemed even remotely embarrassed or regretful about it, either. This morning he had been perfectly cheerful and upbeat as before, even flirtatious as we ate breakfast together.

I wasn't sure how to think about it, to be honest. On the one hand, my mind was on fire with the possibilities – what if there was something more between us than just pure animalistic desire? What if we had a real connection? I had always thought Carter was gorgeous, even back when we were awkward teenagers in high school. Well, more like back when I was an awkward teen. Thinking back, I couldn't recall a single moment during which Carter looked gawky or incompetent. Even when everyone else was going through weird phases and unwieldy growth spurts, Carter had remained handsome and steady. He reminded me of a compass, always reliable, always pointing due north. In a world that was constantly spinning and making messes and complicating things, Carter was the eye of a storm. He was endlessly patient and steadfast. He was honest. He was kind.

He was everything I had ever dreamed of in a man.

But I had to remember I wasn't going to be here in Winchester forever. I still had a life back in the city I would have to return to once this visit was over. I needed to maintain some perspective. After all, I had only been in town for a little while. I couldn't let myself get too caught up in my blossoming feelings for Carter and risk throwing off the real reason I was here: to visit my grandmother and help her out with the renovations.

Of course, I was considerably less nervous about the renovation plans now that I knew Carter was the one in charge. I couldn't help but immediately, instinctively trust him. Especially after seeing how lovely and put together his home was. Clearly he had an eye for this stuff, and I knew he was going to give this project his all. Grandma Nancy was lucky to have him. And even if it was just for one night, so was I.

But for now, there was something else weighing on my conscience: my health. When I was busily firing off emails, putting out ads, and doing the usual grunt work of translation back home, it was easy enough to get caught up in the hustle. I made my own schedule, which meant I could overwork myself to the bone if I so desired. And perhaps it was just out of an undying need to be the best, to prove myself, or maybe it was to distract myself from my wilting social and romantic life, but I had tended to lean toward overworking in recent days. That was another reason for coming home to Winchester – it was a chance to do something different for once, an opportunity to shake things up and escape the monotony of my work. It was a testing ground; if I could handle taking a month off work to visit home, maybe I could handle a bigger trip. Say, that Argentina trip I dreamed about in college, for example. But I had to remind myself to take baby steps. Luckily, Winchester was on the same wavelength in that regard.

Here, the world moved more slowly. People were in no rush to get things done. They kept busy, but not in the frantic, red-eye manner I tended to fall into. No, they followed their passions meticulously, creating beautiful art that spoke to the heart as much as it spoke to their manual abilities. I was impressed and intrigued by the way people around here lived their lives. It had been such a long time since I calmed down and took some time to myself. I missed the way it felt to have a plan in mind, to really take care of my body and feel in tune with my physical and psychological self. I wanted to get back in the swing of things, and as I drove along down the familiar backroads of my adolescence, I knew the gym would be a great first step.

So, I quickly swung by Grandma Nancy's place to swap last night's clothes for a more gym-appropriate outfit, fending off my grand-mother's not-so-subtle questions about where I had spent the night. She was never too pushy, but she was definitely curious.

"Now, I know you're not a child anymore and you can come and go as you please," she began cautiously, "but I still wish you'd tell me who you were with. I worry you know!"

I smiled and paused to pull her into my arms, kissing the top of her curly hair. She giggled and looked up at me with amusement.

"My goodness, you seem to be in a good mood this morning!" She laughed.

"I suppose you could say that," I said, perhaps cryptically.

She put her hands on her hips as I packed a gym bag and slung it over my shoulder. "Where are you off to now?" she asked.

"The gym," I replied. "Just going to sign up and maybe fit in a little cardio. I won't be too long, I promise."

"Oh, take your time, dear. Just check in with me so I know you're all right," she chided gently. I hugged her close again before turning to walk out the door.

Glancing back over my shoulder, I gave her a wink. "Will do, Grandma Nancy."

I got back in the car, feeling really upbeat. I couldn't keep the grin off my face. My tumble in the sheets with Carter last night had put a spring in my step. I rolled down the windows and whistled as I drove, inhaling the fragrant country air. It smelled faintly of jasmine and red clay earth, a familiar scent that never failed to make me feel lighter and happier. I was starting to believe this trip home was a good idea.

I drove straight to the gym and hopped out of my car, those old worries still trying to worm their way into my mind as I approached the entrance. I knew there was a part of me, the old high school version of Mark Sullivan, who was afraid of making a fool of himself. I stepped through the doors of the gym and was immediately hit with the nerve-racking smell of sweat, metal, cleaning solution, and something more obscure I would tentatively describe as just being the scent of pure testosterone. This was the lion's den for me, a place of supreme discomfort. Here, I was surrounded by the kind of natural athlete who would have looked down on me in high school, but I was determined not to let myself backslide. I was here to better myself. I was here to feel good about my body, to increase my strength and take a break from my usual breakneck work pace.

But first I had to find Mason.

Luckily, I didn't have to go far. I rather nervously approached the check-in counter, and a girl with a flouncy blonde ponytail greeted me cheerfully. "Hello! Are you new?" she asked.

I nodded. "Uh, yeah. A friend referred me here. I'm looking for a guy named Mason," I told her.

At just that moment, a tall, impossibly good-looking guy in workout clothes came out of the back office, looking like a marble statue come to life. In one of his hands, he was clutching a dumbbell, which he was curling up and down like it weighed nothing at all. The little metallic number on the side of it said 40. I was intimidated, but he smiled warmly.

"Hey, man. I'm Mason. Who referred you?" he asked.

"A friend of mine. Carter Foster," I answered.

He grinned. "Yeah, yeah! I know him. Great guy. So, would you like to register as a new member, or are you just here for a one-off?" he prompted.

"Well, I was kind of hoping you might be free to help me," I admitted. "Carter said you'd be a big help. I've fallen off the wagon, so to speak, and I want to get back into shape. Take better care of myself, you know."

"Right on," he said, nodding. "I can definitely help with that. Come on. Follow me."

He came out from behind the desk and led me to the back of the gym into a private room filled with workout equipment and a couple of chairs.

"You went to Winchester High, right?" he asked.

"Mhm. Class of 2004," I said.

"Yeah, that sounds right. You look familiar," he said. "I graduated the year before you."

"So you graduated with Carter's class," I reasoned.

"Yep," he said brightly. "He's one of the good guys, for sure. I'm glad he sent you over to me. So tell me, what exactly are you looking to get out of your workouts?"

"Well," I began, shifting uncomfortably, "I just want to be healthier overall. As you might recall, I was a little chubby in high school. Definitely not a natural athlete or anything like that. For a few years, I followed a diet and did some regular cardio workouts. You know, jogging around my block and stuff. But then I kind of... just stopped."

"Mhm. And what happened to make you stop?" he pressed.

"To be honest, it was mostly because of my job. I just got so caught up in working long hours, trying to fit as much work as I could into my days and nights –"

"And nights? You're working days and nights?" he interrupted, looking concerned.

I winced. "Yeah. Sort of. I make my own schedule. I work as a translator. So I kind of stopped going to bed at a reasonable hour. I was going to bed late, getting up early, spending pretty much all my time cramming in as much work as possible."

"Aw, man. That's a common issue people run into these days. That's what's wrong with the world today, you know. Everybody is goin' so fast they don't even take the time to notice time is passin' them by," Mason said sagely.

"You're right. You're totally right." I sighed.

"So, what does your job look like? Are you on your feet at all?" he asked.

I bit my lip. "No. Not really. In fact, my job usually involves me just... kind of sitting in front of my computer for hours and hours. I'm sure that can't be great for my posture and stuff," I admitted.

"That's just about the worst thing you can do for your body, pal," Mason agreed. "But here's the good thing: I can definitely help you get back on track. Of course, it'll be about more than just a workout here and there. I think you need some better structure in your life, Mark. I can help you with that. We can figure out a meal plan and arrange a weekly workout schedule that will give you something to stick to," he explained cheerily.

"Wow. That sounds perfect," I said, impressed.

He clapped me on the shoulder. "Hell yeah, man! I'll get you all sorted out. Don't you worry about a thing. Carter was right to send you over to me. He's a smart dude."

"Yeah, he is," I agreed softly.

"Now, let's talk about what kind of exercise would benefit you the most, all right?" he went on, standing up to pace in front of me. I could tell he was really, truly into his job.

"Sure. Let's get right into it," I said.

"Great! That's what I like to hear!" Mason exclaimed with a big grin on his face. "First of all, you've got to get into a better sleep schedule. No more staying up all night working. Sleep is way more important to overall health and well-being than most people even know. In fact, if you don't get enough sleep, even your metabolism can get all out of whack."

"Wow. That's good to know," I said.

"Yep. It's really important. I know it's hard when you've got a demanding job, but you can't pour from an empty glass, man. You got to look out for yourself first. Treat your body better, and it'll serve you better," he remarked. "So you need to set a time in the evening when you're going to start easing into a sleep routine. That means no more answering work emails after a certain hour, no more forcing yourself to skip meals or put off bedtime for work."

"Damn. How did you know I do all that stuff?" I asked, taken aback.

He laughed. "It's my job, man. I've seen this a hundred times. You're not the only one with these issues. It's more common than you think. And it's easy to fix as long as you've got a little willpower and self-confidence."

"And what if... what if I'm kind of lacking in self-confidence?" I asked.

Mason stopped pacing and looked at me hard. "You'll get there, man. I swear. I'll help you. It won't be easy, but nothing good is easy," he said.

We launched into a full discussion of what I should be eating and drinking, what kind of exercise would be most beneficial for my body type, and how many times a week I should hit the gym. Mason explained that I needed to stick to a high-protein, low-carb diet, less for weight loss and more for just maintaining a healthy routine. He helped me compile a rough meal plan, focusing more on whole foods and less on calorie-counting. We put together a workout routine consisting mostly of cardio – jogging, using the elliptical machine, hiking in the woods, swimming at the public pool. I was relieved to find that every form of exercise he suggested actually sounded kind of fun to me, and the meal plan was more exciting than daunting. I was beginning to understand why Carter had been so adamant about my consultation with Mason. Clearly the guy knew what he was talking about, and he had a unique knack for inspiring motivation in me, even when I was a little nervous.

To get me started, he had me hop on a treadmill. I went at it for half an hour, then jogged around the indoor track and cooled down with some easy stretches. By the end of it, I was feeling both tired out and deeply energized. My blood was pumping, adrenaline was flooding my system, and the rush of endorphins made me feel truly awesome. Mason high-fived me and sent me off to the showers to get cleaned up. As I stood under the hot spray of water, letting it wash away my sweat and grime, my cell phone buzzed in my bag. Thinking it might be my grandmother calling with a question about the renovations, I reached out of the shower and grabbed my phone to answer it.

But to my surprise, when I slid the screen open and said, "Hello," it wasn't Grandma Nancy's voice that responded. Instead, it was Carter.

"Hey, man, how's the gym?" he asked as he grinned.

I couldn't stop myself from smiling. "Oh, hey! It's, uh, it's great. You were right to refer me to Mason. He's fantastic," I said.

"Awesome! I'm so glad I could help. So… anyway, I was calling to ask you a question."

I paused, my heart pounding. "Oh? What is it?" I asked.

"I was wondering if you might want to come over again tonight. I mean, it's totally fine if you don't. I know you've got a lot of stuff going on what with the gym and the renovations and work and –"

"Yes," I blurted out. "Yeah, I would love to come over tonight."

"Oh!" Carter said, sounding a little stunned. "Really?"

"Yeah, of course. It sounds fun," I assured him.

"Cool. Sweet. Awesome," he said, and I could almost hear the smile in his voice.

CARTER

THE MATTRESS CREAKED AS MARK FLOPPED DOWN ONTO IT, LETTING out a breath and spreading his arms out.

"Bed...good..." he joked as I followed him into my room, chuckling.

"Sounds like Mason gave you a hell of a workout," I said, looking him up and down. "You're cute when you're worn out, you know that?"

"Sounds like I'm going to be worn out a lot this month," he said, smiling up at me as I sat down next to him. "I've got to make a meal plan, get my sleep schedule down pat, and hit cardio hard. The more I do it, the easier it'll get. That's always the big hurdle."

"I bet," I said as he sat up, and without being asked, I reached up to his shoulders and started massaging him. "But hey, don't forget to take care of yourself while you're doing this. I'll support you for any life changes you want to make, but I'm not going to sit by and watch you run yourself to death."

"I think it's going to be the opposite problem that gets me, if anything," Mark said, tilting his head back. "But I appreciate it. And this. This is good."

"Glad you're enjoying it as much as me," I flirted, scooting closer to him.

Mark seemed to catch my drift, and I was pleased to find that he relaxed even more for me. I got more adventurous with my massage, rubbing all of his back that I could get to. I was proud of Mark for taking the initiative in this, and I felt an urge to make him feel good that I couldn't resist.

It sure helped that this massage was making *my* cock come to attention, too.

"Tell me this, though," I breathed close to his ear as my hands stroked his hips. "Are you too worn out for a little 'cooldown exercise'?"

Mark looked back at me with hungry eyes, and he swiped his tongue over his lips, tempted. My heart pounded, hoping I hadn't acted too soon, but then he opened his mouth and said those magic words.

"I thought you'd never ask."

I pressed a kiss to his lips from over his shoulder and hugged his body to me as my heart roared in triumph.

I had thought about this a lot. I couldn't deny it. Over the years, my feelings for Mark had never faded, only gone dormant while he was away from my life. But from the second I'd seen him again beside his car, and I'd approached him to give a friendly hello, I knew I wanted him like this. So many things had drifted through my mind involving the two of us that I didn't know where to start. And the more I thought about it, the more I knew it didn't matter where we started.

Our lips broke apart, and we looked at each other in the dim light of my bedroom. My cock pulsed against my rough denim pants to remind me that it needed this sweet, stunning man in front of me, as if I needed a reminder. I reached down to his shirt, and he let me pull it up over his head.

I got a whiff of his faint cologne as I tossed the fabric aside, and I was face-to-face with his naked torso. I licked my lips at the sight of him, every instinct in my body going wild. This was exactly what I had wanted for so long and been denied for stupid reasons. I wasn't about to hold my body back from what it wanted for another second.

My hands went to his sides, and I felt the soft skin, relishing the subtle give of it as my fingers roved over its surface. I went from the sides of his stomach to his back, and I curled my fingers in to drag them back toward the front as I brought my lips to his neck and teased the soft skin between my teeth.

"Oh, fuck," he groaned, and the sound of that husky, hot voice awakened something untamed and hungry deep within me.

I pushed him back onto the bed and straddled him without another moment's hesitation. His scent was all over me, and it was making me crazy for him with each moment we spent together. My hands rubbed his sides as I kissed his neck and let my lips trail down his collarbone, then back up again to his lips. My tongue dove into him, and I felt him exploring me back. His hands went to my ass, and as soon as he got a feel, he tightened his grip and squeezed the cheeks of my ass through the thick pants.

As he did, I took his lower lips between my teeth and grinned, pushing my crotch up against his leg to let him feel my cock throb against him. I wanted him to see what his body did to me, to know exactly how much I was attracted to that gorgeous body of his, no matter what he did with his life or how he looked. Mark was gorgeous, and a few pounds here and there didn't affect how I felt about that. All it did was tell me where to put my hands and what to spend time focusing on.

Mark's hands ventured further up my back, then around my sides and to my front, where he found my belt. He carefully slid it out of the buckle and unbuttoned my pants, and I rewarded him by turning my hips to give him more space to work with. I couldn't keep my hands off him, though, not even for a second. This had been many, many years in the making, and I was not about to let anything come between us.

Once my pants were open, I moved my hips from side to side to help Mark slide them off my legs, exposing my thighs and desperate shaft to the air, and without hesitation, Mark's hand wrapped around my cock. I let out a moan of pleasure to reward him and egg him on. My pants were only halfway down my shins, but I pulled them off the rest of the way myself to encourage Mark to focus on my manhood instead. I knew exactly where I wanted him and how.

He tightened his gentle grip on my cock and moved it up and down my girth. I didn't know a man's hands could be so soft, but I loved how Mark's felt on me. They didn't just stroke my length. They caressed it with such a loving grace that I couldn't help but suspect he had been thinking about this at least as long as I had. And that thought sent a delighted shiver up my back.

But I wasn't here just to fool around with our hands, as much fun as that was. I was here for Mark, and as long as he was willing, I was going to get him.

I pushed his hands away so that I could get my hands on the waist of his pants, and I ran my fingers along the edges, feeling the skin of his stomach pushing against my rough fingers. It brought a smile to my lips, and my stiff cock felt like it was begging me to enter him. And I would, but I wanted to savor this moment.

"Don't think you know just how long I've been thinking about this, Mark," I said in a low, husky tone. "Are you gonna let me do everything I want to do with you? Just say the word, and we can stop this, but I need to know now."

"Carter," Mark breathed, "I wouldn't stop you for anything in the world right now."

I cracked a hungry smile.

"You know the words to make a man's heart melt, you know that?" I growled, and before he could answer, I opened the button of his pants and brought my face down to his crotch.

I took the zipper in my teeth and pulled it down slowly, taking in his masculine scent, and once it reached the bottom, I hooked my fingers in his belt loops and tugged it down. He returned the favor of helping me get his pants down, and as soon as his cock presented itself to me, I fell for the same weakness of him. I couldn't let it stay there unattended, even to get his pants off the rest of the way. I needed to taste it immediately.

My lips went to it, and they found the spot on the underside of his shaft where the crown met the rest of his girth. I pushed my face forward and pinned his cock between the bulge of his stomach and my lips, and I listened to the soft, deep groan that escaped his mouth when I let my tongue push that thick cock and tease the skin I had found. I opened my lips and tasted more of him, and my tongue got more adventurous with each taste. I felt my stubble brush against his skin, and it tickled him the more aggressive I got.

I soon realized I wanted more, so I opened my mouth to take in the crown of his cock. I loved the feeling of covering it in the warmth of my lips and the attention of my tongue. He tasted better than I'd ever dreamed, and I greedily took more of him through my lips. My mouth was pretty big, and I needed every inch of space to take more of him in. I licked the length of his cock from within, alternating between dragging the tip of my tongue from the base all the way up to his crown and massaging the whole length of it with long, broad strokes.

Mark thrust his fingers into my short hair, rubbing my scalp as I claimed his cock for myself, and it thrilled me to feel how much he was enjoying this. Mark had been a guy I wanted to claim for so long, to show him how much I adored his body and his mind, and this was fulfilling every one of those old fantasies with such force that it would have left me weak if I hadn't been energized by his taste.

When I felt a drop of something warm in my mouth, I knew the time had come. I was going to show him what I had wanted for so long, and I was finally going to get it. I slid off him slowly and crawled up to his face again, then cradled his head in my hand while I bent down to press a kiss to his lips.

"Get on your knees for me," I urged him, and he reached up to caress my face.

"Never thought I'd hear you ask," he confessed with that boyish smile I adored so much.

"Never thought I'd have the chance," I shot back with a wink that made Mark blush, and he sat up.

While he turned over and got onto his knees, I went to the nightstand and took out a condom and lube to apply. As I did so, I looked over to Mark and saw him rolling his shoulders back in the dim, sensual light before getting on his elbows and looking back at me. My heart skipped a beat at how goddamn hot that man looked, so vulnerable and hungry for me, right here in my bed. It was art in motion, plain and simple.

I approached him, and I groped his ass. The lube left over on my hands allowed my palms to glide along the surface of his backside as quickly and smoothly as I wished. It made my cock pulse, tightening and begging for touch as it bobbed in front of his cheeks. I readied myself behind him, spread his cheeks, and put the crown of my cock to his tight hole.

Immediately, both our bodies responded as if electricity was running between us in the sweetest possible way. I wanted to thrust my cock deep into him, but I knew I had to take it slowly. I carefully rocked my hips forward just enough to push my tip into him, and I watched his hands grab the sheets tightly.

"How does it feel?" I asked, massaging his ass with my hands while I held my gently throbbing cock in place.

"Fuck, Carter." He grinned. "I knew you would be big, but damn."

"I was thinking the same thing about you." I chuckled, feeling even better about sinking deep into him. "I've got a lot of time to make up for."

"Time's one thing I've got," he said in such an enticing tone that my stomach had butterflies.

My hands went to his hips, and I slid more of me into him, bit by bit. Mark recognized my slow back-and-forth pace, and he matched my motions only enough to help ease me into him. As soon as my entire cock's head was buried in him, a wave of warm feeling rolled up my length and into my crotch. I felt my balls tense in anticipation as I sank into him, and that heat spread up through my body as I let my head fall back, mouth open. The feeling of his tightness around me blew my expectations out of the water, and my expectations had already been high.

Despite not having been with a man before, everything came to me so naturally that I barely knew how to keep up with my instincts. Mark rocked back into me with more boldness as I got further into him, and soon, most of my cock was lodged inside him. I put one hand on his back and used the other to hold his ass and keep groping him as my steady pace turned into soft thrusting, and even that started to pick up more speed in short order.

My chest let out steady grunts as I bucked into Mark, and I heard the same coming from him. The sturdy wooden bed held us up proudly as my knees dug into the mattress. But even so, it wasn't long before my thrusting got strong enough that I heard the thudding of the posts against the wooden walls. I didn't care. In fact, knowing how much force was behind our lovemaking excited me. My cock felt like it was full of sweet fire, urging me to release it, but I wanted to keep teasing both of us to the point that we couldn't stand it anymore.

Once I was happy with my relentless rhythm, I reached around his hips and put my hand around his cock. I was surprised when I felt his hand already there. But rather than pushing his hand away, I let mine interlace with his. Together, we stroked his cock as one, and I felt our fingers get wet from another pulse of precome that spilled out over us.

In that moment, with my cock down to the hilt in him and my hand helping him massage his thick, desperate cock, something struck me. I felt closer to Mark just then than I had ever before, and that feeling washed over me like a comforting blanket that took me by complete surprise. I knew my desires, and I knew how much my manhood had been hungry to feel him, and I even knew that I adored the guy's company more each time we spent time together. But this, this moment of vulnerable safety in each other's company…that was a surprise that made new emotions blossom in me like wild honey-suckle on the side of a mountain trail.

I got lost in him, rutting relentlessly as our hands worked him. What had been low murmurs became breathy, high-paced panting. Neither of us held anything back, and neither of us wanted to slow down. We were going to let all the tension between us build up until our bodies couldn't take it anymore.

JASON COLLINS

And that was exactly what happened.

My wrist almost ached from how I pumped his shaft up and down, brushing my wet thumb over the slit of his cock. I felt my brow glistening as I thrust my hips back and forth, feeling his taut hole hugging the length of my shaft with each new plunge into his ass. At the same time, we both were so overwhelmed with the sensations that we couldn't hold ourselves back any longer.

Both our hands and my hips started to lose that elegant precision we'd been fucking each other with a moment ago, and it gave way to pure instinct, unchecked and ungraceful, but still so wildly beautiful that I couldn't focus on any one thing. My orgasm welled up inside me right as the tip of my cock rubbed against his most sensitive spot deep within him and pushed him across the finish line.

We came together to the sound of my long, relieved moan as I felt a burst of warmth all over our hands. Releasing Mark felt just as sweet and satisfying as my own release, and we massaged each other through the entire process until it was over.

To the sound of our ragged breathing, I slid out of him slowly and carefully, then helped clean us up with a towel hanging at the foot of the bed. With that done, I tossed the towel into the hamper and flopped down beside Mark, smiling up at the ceiling through soft panting before turning my eyes to him. In the afterglow, he looked so beautiful that I couldn't help but wrap my arms around him and kiss his cheek and spoon into him. He hugged me back, laughing softly, and he looked at me with the same lidded eyes and as sloppy a smile as I wore.

"How's that for a cooldown?" I teased him.

"Fuck, that's a regimen I could get used to," he murmured. "But I think I might need a second shower."

"I was hoping you'd say that," I said, sitting up. "Come on, let's get in there. I want to wallow in a steamy bathroom with you for a while."

"Were you reading my mind?" he asked, and I chuckled as I helped him up and hurried to the bathroom with him.

MARK

We were so high up. My heart was pounding, every cell in my body thrumming with strength and awe. Carter was beside me, his fingers interlaced with mine as we floated high above the forest floor. Our feet dangled below us, not even brushing our toes against the prickly branches of pine trees all around. The sky above was a perfect, uninterrupted bright blue in every direction as far as the eye could see. Not a single cloud in sight. The sun glowed so brilliantly that it was difficult to keep my eyes open for long. A smile warmed my face and made my cheeks ache in the best way possible. The forest hummed and trilled with the combined verses of birdsong and musical wind through the trees, every rustle of the breeze sounding like some distant, faintly distorted harp strings. I felt the whole world moving in around me, caressing us and lifting us up and up, through the dense green canopy and up to the sky. A shiver of uncertainty rolled down my spine at the sight of the world falling away below us.

There was a time when this would have terrified me to the core. I used to be afraid of heights. It had happened when I'd climbed a tree alone in the woods at age nine. I'd climbed so high, smiling about how brave I was, about how far my sight would reach if I could only go higher and higher. But I'd gotten stuck there. I hadn't expected it to be scary. I'd sat trembling in the branches like some abandoned baby squirrel, waiting for someone to come rescue me. I had been lucky. My father had ventured out into the forest that evening in search of me when I hadn't come home in time for supper. I'd never missed a meal growing up, so they had known I was in trouble. My father called my name. I could still remember the sound of his deep voice, tinged with worry, echoing through the endless archway of trees. I'd called back, my voice shrill and shaking, barely loud enough to puncture the density of the forest. But he found me. After some coaxing and countless promises that he would catch me, I'd finally slid out of the tree and into my father's waiting arms. We went home, hand in hand, and my mother reheated a plate for me. All was well. I was safe again.

And now, dangling above the world, I clung to Carter's hand like it was a lifeline, the one connection keeping me tethered to the earth. He squeezed it back, and I looked over at him. Relief flooded through my body when I saw that there was no fear in his beautiful eyes. He was smiling. He was happy. And so was I.

His lips parted slowly, meaning burning in his eyes. He was about to say something to me, something important, I could tell. But when he opened his mouth, no words came out. Instead, there was the jarring brrrring brrrring of a telephone, rattling through my brain. Who was calling at this hour, when we were so far above it all? Who could reach through the fog and shake me back to reality? Who could it be...?

My eyes fluttered open, and I squinted at the bright, unearthly glow of the cell phone screen lit up on the nightstand. It took me a few moments to realize I was no longer floating above the tree line with Carter but lying in his bed. And my phone was ringing incessantly. I had forgotten to turn off the sound. Worry gripped my heart. Who would be calling at this hour? The neon-green digital face of the alarm clock told me it wasn't even six in the morning yet. Surely any call before dawn had to be bad news, right? Either way, I didn't want my phone to wake up my gorgeous bedmate, so I promptly rolled over and fumbled for the phone, snatching it and sliding the screen open as I pressed it to my ear.

"Hello?" I answered, my voice sounding scratchy and rough.

"Oh, my dear! You're all right!" chirped the cheerful voice on the other end.

I frowned at my phone, my brain still too muddled to make sense of it all.

"Who...who is calling, may I ask?" I mumbled.

"Why, it's your grandmother. Don't you recognize my voice?" gasped Grandma Nancy.

I smiled to myself and swiped a hand down my face, feeling embarrassed. I slowly pulled myself up to a sitting position in the bed, resting my back against the wooden headboard. I had one hell of a sore body today. Aches and pains flared all over me, reminders of the workouts I had been engaged with lately, both in the gym and in this very bed.

"Sorry, Grandma. It's just early, that's all. I'm not totally awake yet," I told her.

"Are you okay, my love?" she asked.

"Yeah, of course. Why wouldn't I be?" I said confusedly.

"Well, because you never came home last night again. At least, it didn't seem like you came by at all during the night. I worried you might have gotten into a car accident or fallen asleep at the wheel or something," she rambled.

I blanched, feeling guilty for worrying her. Especially at her age, the last thing she needed was a serious fright. I sighed, noticing that my whispered conversation was causing Carter to wake up. I could see the faint outline of his body stirring under the sheets, even in the low light of the cell phone glow.

"My apologies, Grandma Nancy. I should have told you what was going on. I swear, I didn't mean to upset you," I assured her.

"Oh, don't worry about that, dear. I just wanted to hear your voice and make sure you were, you know, alive and well," she replied.

"Why are you awake this early?" I asked suddenly.

She chuckled. "Well, when you get to my age, you realize the importance of making every day count. So I like to get up early and watch the sunrise. Who knows how many more years of sunrises and sunsets I will get? So I try to catch as many as I can," she explained sagely.

"Aw, come on. You're not that old," I chided her gently. "But I know what you mean. That's an admirable idea. I usually miss the sunrise because I sleep in too late."

"I know. You're young, still. Sorry for waking you like this. I was just frightened when I got up and checked your room and saw you weren't there. So I feel like I ought to ask: where are you, dear?" Grandma Nancy inquired pointedly.

I looked over at Carter, who was slowly waking up now. My heart surged with affection to see his gorgeous eyes blinking blearily in the soft light. He looked positively dreamy, his eyes half-lidded and his hair all tousled and messy. I wanted nothing more than to toss my phone aside and scramble back under the sheets with him. I could feel the cozy warmth radiating off of him, and I wanted to steal some of it for myself.

He mouthed the words *good morning,* and I nodded, unable to keep from smiling.

"Mark?" my grandmother prompted me again.

"Oh! Right. Sorry. I'm just at a…a friend's place," I lied awkwardly.

Carter raised an eyebrow, looked amused. He mouthed the words *a friend?* I waved my hand at him and looked away. He was too distracting.

"A friend? Oh, which one?" Grandma Nancy asked enthusiastically.

"A, uh, close friend," I said. "Very close. Yep."

"*Oh,*" she said meaningfully. "Are you…are you still in bed?"

I could feel my face flushing deep crimson at that question. The last thing I wanted to do right now was discuss my sex life with my grandmother. So I quickly tried to change the subject.

"No. Nope. Not anymore. I've gotten up, and I'm getting dressed," I told her, even though I made no move to get up at all. Carter was now doing everything in his power to stifle a laugh while I blushed deeper and deeper.

"Wait a second," Grandma Nancy said suddenly and then gasped.

"What kind of friend are you with right now? A friend-friend or a boyfriend?"

Oh god. Nope. This was not happening. I was definitely not awake enough to have this kind of conversation with my sweet grandmother.

"Can we please not discuss this right now?" I said sharply.

But she was already running far ahead of me with this one.

"Is it someone I know? Are you going on dates, Mark? Are you fallin' in love? Oh! Wouldn't that just be so wonderful?" she gushed.

I hoped to god that Carter couldn't hear her.

"Shh. No. Grandma, you're getting ahead of yourself –" I tried to protest, but she wasn't having it at all.

"What's his name? How did you meet? Is it serious?" she bombarded me.

I could clearly hear the grin in her voice. I pictured her bouncing up and down excitedly on the balls of her feet as she often did when she was enthused about something. I supposed maybe it was at least nice to know she cared so deeply about my personal life, but it didn't make it any less awkward.

"Yes, you know him. We met back in high school. No, it's nothing serious," I said.

Carter pulled a theatrical pouting face that made me snort-laugh.

"Oh! Oh! Can I guess? Is it that boy you used to play in the marchin' band with? Oh, what was his name?" she murmured thoughtfully.

"Alex? No. Not at all. Stop trying to guess," I said hastily.

"Oh my goodness. I know who it is!" she gasped. "It's Carter, isn't it?"

I closed my eyes and heaved a sigh. There it was. Carter sat up next to me in bed, a big grin across his face. I shook my head and mouthed *I'm sorry*, but he simply looked amused.

"Am I right? Is it him?" my grandmother said excitedly.

"Yes, Grandma Nancy. You guessed right. I'm with Carter. Can we just let it go?" I said.

"Let it go? Why on earth would we do that? I simply adore Carter!

Why don't you boys get all tidied up and head on over here?" she suggested brightly.

"Well, I don't know about that," I said. She breezed right past my hesitation.

"Come on, love. It'll be wonderful. I'm already plannin' to cook up a big, hearty Southern breakfast for the construction boys when they get here, so you might as well join us," she said matter-of-factly.

"Grandma, you know you're already paying those guys. You don't have to feed them, too," I reminded her.

"Well, of course I don't have to, but I want to! It's always so lovely gettin' to cook for a big group. You're all still growin', and you need your nutrition, you know," she said.

Carter was nodding fervently, urging me to accept the invitation.

I sighed and pinched the bridge of my nose. "All right. Okay. Fine. You got us. We'll come over for breakfast," I relented.

"Oh, how wonderful! I'm so excited," she chimed.

"Should we bring anything or...?" I trailed off.

"Just yourselves, of course! I've got it all under control. Just come back to the house whenever you're ready and make sure you let me know when you're on the way so I can get started on the cooking, okay?" she chirped.

"Are you sure? That's a lot of men to cook for, Grandma," I said.

"No excuses! I'm doing this. Now, you two boys get all cleaned up and decent!"

I winced. "Okay. We'll see you in a bit, then," I gave in.

"Lovely. See you soon!" she said and promptly hung up.

"Your grandmother is one hell of a character," Carter remarked.

"Yeah. I know. Trust me." I sighed.

He leaned over and kissed me on the cheek, sending shivers of delight through my body.

"It's adorable. I really like that woman. She's got a big heart," he said. His words made me feel all warm and tingly inside. My grandmother was one of the most important people in the world to me, and to know that Carter so genuinely adored her was encouraging.

"She's great," I agreed. "But I wish she would've called a little later.

Sorry I woke you up so early. We don't have to get up yet, of course. We can wait."

"Nah, I'm already awake and thinkin' about that big country breakfast. Might as well get up and at 'em, you know?" Carter said cheerily.

He swung his legs over the side of the bed and stood up, stretching like a cat. My mouth nearly watered at the sight of his muscles tensing and flexing. God, he was gorgeous.

"You know you don't have to go, right? She's my grandmother, so of course I'm going to show up for stuff like this, but you're the contractor. She's got you on the payroll to renovate her house. It's early. It's rainy outside. You have a million excuses not to go if you don't want to," I reminded him, just to be sure.

But he just smirked at me with amusement.

"Well, I appreciate your concern, Mark. But honestly, I would love to go. I wouldn't dream of missin' out on an opportunity for free Southern cooking." He chuckled. "Especially from a sweet lady like your grandmother. Nobody knows how to cook like her. That's for damn sure."

"You sound pretty certain about that," I said with a smile.

He came around to my side of the bed and reached for my hands to pull me up to my feet. Then he pulled my arms around his waist so that our bodies were flush up against one another. My heart raced at the simple sensation of his hard, powerful body, sculpted by years of manual labor and good eating, pressed to mine. He was impossibly warm to the touch, and there was a familiar, homey, musky scent to his skin that was intoxicating to me. I wished that I could bottle it. I tilted my head back to gaze up into his handsome, smiling face. Everything about him was perfect. I could hardly believe that this was my reality – that I was really standing here in the bedroom of this gorgeous guy with my arms wrapped around his muscular frame, the sun just starting to rise and illuminate the room in pillars of soft golden light. Carter grinned down at me and kissed me softly on the forehead.

"Come on," he urged me gently. "Let's hop into the shower. I think we could both use a little help waking up this morning."

"Sounds perfect to me," I agreed.

He led me by the hand to the bathroom down the hall, humming some vaguely familiar tune under his breath as we went. He switched on the shower and turned back to softly kiss me while we waited for the water to heat up. Carter glanced at our reflection in the mirror and chuckled quietly.

"What? What is it?" I asked.

"Oh, nothin'. Just that you and I make one damn handsome pair." He laughed. "Who would've ever seen it coming?"

"You and me? Nobody. I certainly never saw it," I admitted.

"Why is that?" he asked as he parted the shower curtain and stepped into the steamy tub. I followed after him, contemplating my answer and how to word it properly.

"Well, it's just that…you know," I said with exasperation. "You're this gorgeous, strong Adonis, and I'm just Mark."

He chuckled and pulled me close so that we were both standing under the warm, comforting stream of water. Beads of hot water rolled down over his shoulders and strong chest, his hair getting dark and damp by the second.

"You're more than 'just' anything to me. You're a good man, Mark Sullivan. Anybody would be lucky to have you, for however long it lasts," he remarked.

"I just worry sometimes I might not be good enough, you know?" I opened up.

Carter looked at me hard for a moment. "Why's that?" he asked.

I stared down at our feet bashfully. "You and I didn't exactly run in the same circles back in high school, Carter. You were always one of the popular guys. The hot guys. And then there was me. Chubby and insecure. Never on your level," I admitted.

He tilted my chin up and kissed me gently. "You know what I see when I look at you?"

"What?" I asked.

Carter grinned. "An ambitious, successful, hard-working, compassionate guy with an amazing job, a good head on his shoulders, a big heart, and a lot of patience. I see a guy who has made something of himself in the world and yet is still humble enough to come home to a small town like Winchester to spend time with his grandmother. That's who I see. And from where I'm standing, that makes you the total package, Mark," he said softly.

I couldn't stop blushing. "You're far too kind to me," I said.

He shook his head. "Nah. I'm just tellin' the truth," he insisted.

"I guess growing up around here, it was hard to see myself that way," I said. "Don't get me wrong. I love my family. They always treated me like I was perfect as I was. But at school, the other kids could be...insensitive. You know what I mean?"

Carter looked a little regretful. "Yeah. I know."

"And I guess, no matter how many years have passed, no matter how successful I feel, some of that old mess still bothers me sometimes," I said with a shrug.

"That's understandable," he said. "But the next time you start thinkin' you might not be amazing, I want you to push those rude thoughts right out of your head. Because you're a good one, Mark. And I like you. A lot."

I blushed and leaned into him. "I like you a lot, too, Carter," I told him truthfully. "I just want to make sure I'm good enough for a guy like you. For however long I'm here. And I guess I worry that eating big country breakfasts like Grandma Nancy makes might ruin what progress I've been making."

"Well, then, we'll just have to find some ways to burn off the extra calories, huh?" Carter insinuated slyly.

He gave me a wink and leaned in to kiss me more passionately this time, his hand sliding up to tangle in my damp hair. My cock twitched and throbbed between my legs as we rutted against one another, moaning and clutching for purchase under the slick shower spray. We spent the next half hour kissing, groping, feeling each other up. We basked in the steamy warmth of the shower, waking up each other with fervent kisses until finally his cock was stiff and sliding up and down alongside mine, both of us gasping and caught up in shared pleasure. We lazily embraced, taking our time as we mounted higher and higher, closer to the edge. Finally, we came together, shuddering with the residual waves of bliss. Exhilarated and relieved, we held each other as the slick come slipped down our legs and down the drain. Then we slowly lathered up, rinsed off, and got out of the shower, ready to face the day side by side.

CARTER

To say I hadn't expected to be driving to a work site with Mark driving behind me after a steamy night and sweet morning with him would be an understatement. I felt bad that we had to take separate vehicles, even. I couldn't get enough of the guy. At each stop light we came to on the way to Miss Nancy's house, I found myself glancing in the rearview mirror at him. I wasn't exactly staring longingly (not that I didn't want to) but seeing him doing his own thing and watching how he carried himself was interesting and exciting. He was a breath of fresh air I hadn't been expecting, nor had I realized how much I needed him around.

I was still glowing after our night together. I could hardly believe it had happened. I hadn't just slept with Mark, but I had gotten him to stay the night again and had what felt like a couple of perfect mornings with him. And as far as I was concerned, those perfect mornings could keep coming, and I would be happy as a clam.

He was proving to be a tough one to figure out. When I'd first met him again, it had seemed to me like he had life pretty solidly figured out. At least, that's what I'd figured when I'd been able to clear my head of thoughts of him in my bed. He had a solid job with flexible hours, he lived somewhere he seemed to like, he had a good relationship with his family, and he looked incredible. Best of all, he was a caring guy who genuinely worried about his family's well-being and wanted the best for them. That was a rare thing, in my experience.

It bothered me a little to see him feeling so self-conscious about his weight. I was always happy to see people wanting to improve themselves, so I would gladly stand by him and help him get his life a little more organized and healthy if that was what he wanted. But the one thing that did concern me was the idea that Mark might think I didn't find him attractive.

That was so outlandish that I could have laughed about it.

I found Mark hot any way he was, and I wanted him to know it. If that just meant I had to keep *showing* it until he got the message, that was fine by me, I thought to myself with a quiet chuckle. The rest of the trip to Miss Nancy's house was filled with my daydreaming about taking him on a trip to one of my favorite fishing spots, and before I knew it, we were pulling up at the house.

I was pleased to see that the landscapers were already at work in the yard, digging out the pond. A backhoe was sitting idly next to an excavated crater in the ground with nobody attending it, and the trucks parked by the curb told me a few others were already on-site. Not all of these people answered directly to me. In fact, most didn't. As the general contractor, I had a managerial role in the project as a whole, and I brought together the supervisors of all the actual construction workers on the site.

Of course, in a town like Winchester, you still got to know everyone and the work environment so well that we might as well have all worked for the same people. Winchester only broke a population of 2,000 on a good year, so when a group of guys entered the workforce, you tended to know most of them on a first-name basis, even if you weren't necessarily rubbing shoulders with them on the regular.

"We're not late, are we?" Mark said as he climbed out of his car and crossed the yard to walk up to the steps of the house with me. "I didn't realize people were going to be here so soon."

"Nah, smell that in the air?" I said, grinning. "We're right on time.

The guys have been here since early in the morning, and Miss Nancy is already up at dawn anyway."

"Oh god, I can practically taste the butter in the *air*," Mark said, laughing even though his face looked vaguely pained.

"Dairy farmers make a killing off Winchester, that's for sure." I chuckled, approaching the door.

"Hey, before we go in there," Mark said just as I was reaching for the door, and I turned to look at him with a raised eyebrow. "This is going to sound weird but bear with me."

"Sure thing, man, shoot!" I said with a smile.

"Do you think you could...'have my back' in there with the food situation?" he asked, screwing up his face as he tried to figure out how precisely to word the request.

"Have your back?" I asked, tilting my head to the side. "I've always got your back, but I'm not sure what you mean."

"All I'm saying is, there's going to be a *lot* of biscuits, gravy, honey butter, and pancakes coming out hot in that kitchen," he said as if we were about to head into a war zone. "And I don't know how many meals you've had with my grandma, but turning down food isn't going to be the easiest thing in the world. As much as I can appreciate a hearty breakfast..."

"...Ohhh," I said at last, nodding in understanding. "I hear you. All right, I don't know how much extra I'll be able to pack down, but I hear you loud and clear. Exercise plan or no, Winchester boys take care of each other. Now let's get in there, or there won't be anything left."

"Sounds good," Mark said, looking encouraged, and we headed inside together.

We opened the door to a wave of warmth, the sounds of friendly chatter from further inside the house, and the overwhelming aroma of simply everything that a woman like Miss Nancy could have up her sleeve to handle breakfast for a small group of men. And that translated to a hell of a lot of food. *Bannister Heights* was playing on the TV, which was hardly a surprise. Miss Nancy owned a few seasons on DVD. I guess she was a fan. She was probably an admirer of the handsome rogue Adrian Bannister, and more specifically, his heartthrob actor Jesse Blackwell. As we walked through the living room, he was confessing his hidden love for his best friend's beautiful young widow.

There was no need to knock or announce ourselves, of course. Everyone knew each other in Winchester so well that most older folks still had trouble getting into the habit of locking their doors at night. All we had to do was put a couple of bodies in seats, and we'd get stuffed full. The two of us made our way back to the kitchen, and we were greeted with a sight that did my heart good.

The three workers already seated at the table were familiar faces. They had their hard hats off and sleeves rolled up, hands washed as clean as they could get with lifestyles like ours. Two of them were Bob and Peter from the landscaping company, and the other was Adam, a carpenter I had worked with in the past, probably here to get things started on the porch. But the three of them weren't what drew my eye in first. Mark's gaze was already locked on the main event.

Miss Nancy spun around at the stove to look at us triumphantly, with an almost ominous glint in her eye as she crossed her arms and smiled proudly at us.

"About time y'all got here," she chided us playfully. "I was about to have the boys here bring some food over to your place!"

"Wouldn't miss it for the world, Grandma." Mark chuckled as we surveyed the food that was spread out on the stove, the counter, the oven, and the table already.

The first thing that caught my eye was what Miss Nancy took out of the oven, basking all of us in a mouthwatering aroma: thick, tall, buttery biscuits that were still glistening on the flaky, golden brown surfaces as she set them on the stovetop with loving care. Every single one of them would have been enough to keep a man satisfied for an hour or so at least. Next to it was a saucer holding what was going to be the crowning finisher on each one of the biscuits. It was gravy, and not just any gravy, but Grandma Nancy's gravy. She loaded the stuff so thick with sausage that calling it a gravy anymore was debatable, depending on which diner you were eating at. Soon, each one of those mounds of light and fluffy bread would be smothered in enough sausage to kill a man and garnished with the slightest amount of chives for a little color.

Speaking of sausage, there was already a massive plate on the warmer piled high with sausage and eggs. The sausage links were stuffed so full that they looked about ready to burst, and the drops of savory moisture on them made the ensemble look like it was begging to be bitten into. The sausages were being invaded by a mountain of scrambled eggs, all golden yellow and cooked to perfection, dotted with black pepper and ready to be adorned with the best hot sauce in town, a local brand that perfectly captured the flavor of proudly grown local hot chilis without overwhelming the flavor with heat. The pile of protein was giving off a rich aroma that I had smelled from halfway across the yard.

No Southern breakfast would be complete without grits. I watched Miss Nancy stick a wooden spoon into that pot and stir the mixture, and when she did, it showed off a wave of the grainy porridge-like food that was swimming in so much butter the whole thing had a vibrant goldenrod color, and then she added the cheddar cheese. It melted almost instantly, swirling into the waves of grits that were absolutely laden with fat shrimp that had taken on their share of the butter in the pot.

"Why don't you two have seats, and I'll get you all fixed up," she said with a wink, gesturing to the table where a couple of empty seats were waiting for us.

Mark and I exchanged a glance and nodded to each other, a silent reminder that I was going to help Mark navigate this minefield of rich foods one way or another. And that was going to be easier said than done...because what we had seen so far wasn't anywhere close to all the food she had made.

She fanned the biscuits as they cooled, then set to prying them all out with a fork and setting them aside for the moment. Mark's eyes went wide when she opened the oven *again* to carefully take out a cast iron skillet with none other than Miss Nancy's famous cornbread, and she set it on the stovetop next to three different flavors of homemade preserves: strawberry, peach, and apple.

I turned my head to point that out to Mark, but his attention was on the middle of the table. There was already a plate of blueberry muffins set out with a few of them missing, suggesting the guys had already been hard at work putting some of them away as a pre-break-fast snack.

"Don't fill up too soon," Miss Nancy said over her shoulder as she opened the fridge and took out a massive tray of what I was correct in assuming was banana pudding, the thick and hearty kind you could only get from a Southern household. "I still have some ham and redeye gravy to add to the spread. Oh, and I almost forgot the pancakes!"

"I think Miss Nancy might just be out to kill us all before we get started," I said to the other guys with a grin, and they laughed along with Mark.

"Oh, don't you worry about that," she said with a grin as she bustled over to pour us mugs of piping hot coffee. "If I wanted y'all dead, I'd just have you over for Thanksgiving."

"She isn't kidding," Mark warned me with a knowing smile.

Plates came out in waves, and if the kitchen table hadn't been made right here in Winchester, I would have been worried it wouldn't be sturdy enough to hold everything. Miss Nancy laid out empty plates for everyone, and every plate of food had large serving spoons and spatulas stuck into the food itself.

"Help yourselves, everyone," she invited us proudly. "Don't be shy! They're gonna come smash up the kitchen in the morning, so this is the last chance I'll get to cook this much for y'all in a few weeks! You had better believe I'm gonna ride the time for all it's worth."

"Leftovers to last you a month, Miss Nancy?" I asked as I went for the biscuits and doused one in gravy.

"Oh, sweetie, you ain't even seen what I've got up my sleeves." She laughed. "Just you wait 'til I get through with lunch and dinner for today. I'll have leftovers for the whole neighborhood. And if you don't think we'll have us a low country boil sometime this month, just you wait and see, young man."

"Yeah, I'm thinking our leg of the work might just take all month," Bob joked casually, stretching out at the table and making himself comfortable as the rest of us laughed.

"Besides, I've gotta make up for Mark here being subject to city eatin' for so long," she added. "I don't know how he survives up there with the kinds of things they eat!"

"It's all right, but it doesn't hold a candle to home," Mark admitted, grinning at the sumptuous feast before him. "Honestly, I'm surprised I can hold on to this weight as it is."

"You know, when I was a little girl and my mama first told me 'Nancy, the only certain things in life are death and taxes', I just said, 'Well, then I guess we ought to at least add good food to the list and make life worth livin'!'" she said, and the murmur of general approval from everyone at the table signaled the beginning of breakfast.

As soon as Miss Nancy's back was turned to us, Mark gave me a look, and I gave him a quick nod. We piled our plates with food, but we did so with purpose. Mark and I were sitting side by side, so he put the carb-heavy foods on the half of the plate closest to me, and he put the protein-heavy eggs and sausage and bacon on the far end from me. I caught on to what he was doing and started mirroring how I laid out the food on my plate.

Out of everything that was on the spread right then, the meats and eggs were the most nutritious things available for what Mark wanted to do with his workout routine, so that was what he would focus on. That, and maybe the ham.

The other construction guys were so focused on devouring their food immediately that we were free to connive in relative privacy. We only had to keep an eye on Miss Nancy and make sure she didn't turn around in time to catch on to what we were doing. I scarfed down my sausage and gravy-laden biscuit, but as soon as she turned her head, Mark nudged his biscuit to the edge of the plate and flitted his eyes from it to me, meaningfully. To me, depriving an honest man of his right to one of Miss Nancy's homemade biscuits was a crime against humanity, but if that was how Mark wanted me to help him, then by god, I would shovel down another biscuit.

I burned through so many calories in my day-to-day life that it didn't make a bit of difference to me, just like the rest of the work crew at the table.

Our method worked like a charm. I could eat like a wolf when I wanted to, and this morning was no exception. We only hit a snag when I was trying to surreptitiously take a pancake from Mark's plate and Adam noticed me trying to trade him for a sausage link. Adam made eye contact with me while Miss Nancy's back was turned. At the same moment that he quirked an eyebrow at me, I put a finger to my lips and glanced at Nancy. Adam looked confused for a moment, then smiled in understanding and nodded, chuckling.

There was still a lot of overeating happening here; that was unavoidable. But Mark seemed to be happy to channel that into excess protein to put to work later today, ideally once he had time to let the food digest a little. Honestly, Mark got off easy. By the end of the meal, I must have put away enough food to feed two of *me*.

"Oh, I need to get renovations done more often if that's what it takes to get a room full of people who appreciate my cooking." Miss Nancy chuckled at the end of the meal, looking around at the war zone of empty plates and stuffed men, most of us leaning back in our chairs and holding a hand over our guts in various states of defeat. I was pretty sure Bob had tried to unbutton his pants at the table without anyone noticing, at some point.

"No, see, this is intentional," Mark said with a teasing grin on his face, leaning forward at the table. "She shows you what she can do with an old kitchen so it'll inspire you to make the new one even better."

"Don't give away my secrets!" Miss Nancy laughed, brandishing a wooden spoon.

"Really though, I appreciate it," Mark said with a warm smile, and the rest of the table echoed its deepest gratitude.

Nobody could bring a group of people together quite like a grandma could, and Miss Nancy was an expert. She joked around as much as Mark did, but it was clear that she really got some serious satisfaction out of things like this.

"And with that, I need to go put this protein to good use with Mason," Mark said, standing up slowly.

"I'll see you out," I said, "but I've got to hang back here and touch base with Adam on a few things for the porch."

"Don't work yourself to death, sweetie," Miss Nancy said, bustling over to hug Mark.

"I'll try." Mark chuckled, and we headed to the front door, where we had a moment's privacy again.

I immediately leaned in to steal a quick kiss from Mark, which made him blush, and he squeezed my hand.

"Hey, thanks for the help back there," he whispered with a wink. "Good thing the kitchen's going to be under construction for the next few weeks, or this workout would be a lost cause."

"I hear that." I chuckled. "But don't brush off your grandma's advice, either. Be careful out there."

"You don't have to worry about that," he assured me, and he pecked me on the cheek before opening the door. "Catch you later!"

My heart was fluttering as I made my way back to the kitchen, where I was surprised to find the entire room giving me the smuggest smirks I'd ever seen. I arched an eyebrow, smiling slowly and looking around at everyone.

"What?"

"You two," Miss Nancy said, "are sweeter than molasses. That's all I'm gonna say!"

"Put 'er here, Casanova," Adam said, raising a hand to give him a high five as I slowly realized that the entire room had been in on the spark between Mark and me.

I couldn't keep a smile off my face as I rolled my eyes...but neither could I leave Adam hanging. I clapped my hand to his, then teasingly hit him on the arm as we all got up and cleaned up the kitchen before getting started on a hard day of work.

MARK

I FELT LIKE I WAS FLOATING A HUNDRED MILES ABOVE THE EARTH. THE smile on my face seemed permanently stuck there, my spirits soaring higher and higher as I walked briskly down the front steps of Grandma Nancy's place and down to the driveway. I whistled low under my breath, swinging my keyring around my finger. My heart was pounding like crazy, just from that quick stolen kiss from Carter. I didn't know what kind of magic that man had in his touch, but it was something awfully powerful. All it took was a glance from those gorgeous eyes or the faintest brush of his fingertips over my skin, and I was hooked. Entranced. Hanging on his every word, his every move-ment. I was falling for him, and I was falling hard.

Normally, that would have been a terrifying realization to come to. After all, I was usually very cautious – maybe even overly cautious – especially when it came to sex and romance. I could count my number of partners on one hand, and not because I was particularly prudish or anything like that. It was just that I guarded my heart fiercely. Sometimes I thought it might be yet another side effect of growing up as a sort of outsider kid, the bullied kid.

My childhood hadn't been hugely traumatic in any way, and for the most part I had felt safe and loved. My family had always looked out for me, so even if kids had been rude to me at school, I had always been able to count on waiting for that final bell of the day to ring so I could go home to my safe haven. But still, there had been times during the school day when I'd felt as though I had to put on several layers of armor just to get through the difficult moments. I'd learned that wearing my heart on my sleeve just made me more vulnerable, an easier target for those bitter bullies who would pick off the weakest member of the proverbial herd. I'd learned to keep quiet, to hide my true feelings behind a thick brick facade, make myself as small and unobtrusive as possible.

I'd retreated to places where I felt safe – books and movies and television shows. It had partly been my interest in foreign cinematography that had gotten me into learning other languages, actually. I'd studied history and architecture and culture, spending endless hours researching for fun. So in a way, I had my uncomfortable adolescence and long hours spent alone in my room to thank for my current career in translation, as well as my dream goal of someday backpacking in Argentina. I didn't want anybody to see me for who I was, not even my closest friends. It took some time after I'd graduated and moved away for me to rediscover the wealth of emotions and desires I had kept so tightly restrained all those years in school.

Nowadays, I was more in touch with my feelings, of course, but there was still a veil of protection separating me from total head-over-heels twitterpation. But I could feel my emotions tugging at the seams, threatening to burst free in an explosion of bright color and feelings. That had a lot to do with Carter. He was so unapologetically Carter, so unabashed in the way he pursued the things he loved – in and out of bed – that he encouraged me to look at things the same way. He was authentic. He was real. And he was not even the slightest bit afraid of what might happen, of who might be watching and judging his actions. I admired that about him, even though it also kind of frightened me. I was simultaneously intimidated and emboldened by his outward shows of affection. Carter held nothing back, and I was learning, however slowly, to do the same.

And of course, seeing the way he interacted with my beloved

grandmother certainly had an effect on me, too. He was so patient and genuine, even when she was being pushy about something. She clearly adored him, which was also a good sign, as my grandmother had always been a pretty accurate judge of character. I could still remember one time in high school when my cousin had started dating this guy none of us really liked. But Grandma Nancy had hated him. She had taken every possible opportunity to inform my cousin that her boyfriend wasn't trustworthy. My cousin was eighteen at the time, freshly graduated from high school and self-assured in her choices in the way only a barely legal adult could feel. She had gone right on ahead with the engagement once he proposed to her. She'd even started planning a wedding. We all hadn't seen a point in arguing with her and had gone along with the plans. Except Grandma Nancy. She'd continued to suspect he was something other than what he proclaimed to be.

Needless to say, months later he'd revealed himself to be a bit of a con artist. He had been caught stealing money from my cousin's bank account to funnel into his gambling habit, and luckily my cousin found out about all that before the wedding could go through. Grandma Nancy had had a gigantic "I-told-you-so" for us all after that. She had somehow known all along.

So when she liked somebody, really liked somebody, it meant something. And she sure as hell seemed to adore Carter. It made my heart swell with pride to think about it.

On top of my grandmother's shining brand of approval, Carter's even-keeled personality was oddly comforting to me. Like any catastrophe that might happen would still be within the realm of something he could fix. Maybe that was what made him such a fantastic contractor; he saw the world as a series of things to be fixed up and perfected rather than a jungle of worries and pitfalls like I sometimes saw. I wondered if there was anything he couldn't do. So far, he appeared to be utterly unflappable, totally put together in every way. No wonder he'd been so popular in high school. Carter was the epitome of a Southern gentleman, even though he was more like a Carolina bobcat in bed.

I blushed to myself as I slid into my car and turned on the engine. The put-putting of the engine reminded me yet again of Carter's straightforward way of handling my car battery situation. He was a fixer in every sense of the word. He presented the solution to a problem matter-of-factly, without expecting an avalanche of praise in response. That was amazing to me, and proof that he was, in fact, a true gentleman. He'd seen that I needed a jump, so he jumped my car. He'd seen that I needed a battery, so he brought me one. He'd seen that I needed backup and support to get through Grandma Nancy's smorgasbord of buttery, bacon-greasy breakfast foods, so he backed me up and supported me. It was simple. It was easy. And it was hot as hell.

I couldn't deny that I was attracted to him, body, mind, and soul. Whenever I was with him, it felt like my insecurities were miles away. I could still see them, and every now and again they would come creeping back up on me, trying to sneak their way back in. But then Carter would kiss me with those perfect lips or say my name in that syrupy, delicious Southern drawl that got me so hot around the collar, and everything would go back to normal again. He chased away my fears without even having to try. I felt safe with him, and that was a new feeling for me.

I never wanted it to end.

But I had to remind myself this was all temporary. It was just a fun little hometown fling, something to keep me busy and work out my body while I was here in town visiting. Eventually I would have to return to my place in the big city, go back to that version of Mark Sullivan. At least maybe I could go back to it feeling brighter and lighter with a spring in my step. Maybe Carter was the retreat I needed. Maybe he could rejuvenate my soul and send me packing back to the city with an adjusted optimism that would make my days seem less daunting. That was all I could hope for, right?

Still, for now at least, it felt good to pretend this could be something real. One thing was for certain: lots of things had changed drastically since my high school days, and I counted myself lucky in that regard. Some people got stuck in that adolescent mindset forever, and

I was happy not to be a part of that group. I was an adult, I was getting my health and fitness back on track, and I was spending every bit of free time with the sexiest guy I had ever known. I kind of wished I could go back in time and visit high-school Mark just to tell him what he had to look forward to.

I couldn't stop smiling as I drove to the gym. I felt refreshed and ready for a hard workout, especially since I'd eaten all that protein at breakfast. For once, I felt energized after a meal instead of sluggish and tired. Surely my determination to get into shape was part of it, but I couldn't pretend like Carter wasn't a main defining factor, too. I wanted to be better for myself, but I also wanted to be better for him. He kept me accountable, just like Mason did, and I was bound to see some good results. I was confident about that. As I drove, I turned on the radio, for once not grimacing at the fact that all the local radio stations played country music. Maybe it was just because I was so drawn to Carter's Southern accent (he made it sound so damn good) but for some reason, the music didn't annoy me today. It just made me smile.

I pulled the car into the lot in front of the gym and turned off the engine, reaching into the back seat to grab my gym bag. I hummed a country tune softly as I walked across the parking lot and into the gym, unable to wipe the smile from my face. I was greeted almost instantly by Mason, who was hanging around the front reception desk chatting with the young woman there. Mason grinned and waved at the sight of me.

"Oh, hey! Good morning, man," he said, leaning in to shake my hand. "You ready for a killer workout?"

"Actually, yes. I'm looking forward to it," I said truthfully.

"You two have way more enthusiasm than anybody should at this hour," the girl in the swivel chair remarked. I noticed she was holding her forehead in her hand, her face scrunched up into a grimace.

Mason chuckled and rolled his eyes. "It's closer to noon than morning, Kate," he pointed out. She just sighed and closed her eyes.

"I know. But still, the fluorescent lights are torture on my eyes right now," she groaned.

Mason gave me a wink. "Kate here is a little bit hungover if you can't tell," he said.

"Mason! Don't go telling customers stuff like that! Jeez," she protested.

I chuckled. "Hey, I'm not judging. I've definitely been there," I told her.

She managed to crack one eye and force a smile. "Thanks. I guess I just can't handle my liquor like I used to," she lamented dramatically.

"Kate, you're twenty-three years old. You can handle anything." Mason laughed. Then he clapped his hands and looked at me intently. "All right. Enough chitchat. Let's leave Kate to her hangover and get started, yeah?" he prompted.

"Yep. Sure. Let's go," I agreed.

"Have fun," Kate murmured, her voice muffled by her hands cradling her face.

Mason came around and gestured for me to follow him. "Come on. I've got a new idea in mind for us today," he said.

"What's that?" I asked, following him.

He glanced back over his muscular shoulder and said, "Yoga!"

"Really? Yoga?" I repeated incredulously.

He laughed. "Hey now, don't knock it till you've given it a fair shake," he said.

"But isn't that, like, pretty tame?" I said.

"You'd be surprised. Some of those poses get pretty intense. You'll definitely still work up a sweat. Besides, you're not just here to work out your body. You've got to get your mind on track, too, or it's a waste of time," Mason explained wisely.

"Huh. I guess that makes sense," I relented.

He led me into a private room and laid out two cushy yoga mats on the shiny floor.

"I have a confession to make," I said nervously. "I, uh, can't even touch my toes."

Mason grinned. "No problem. I can barely touch them, and I'm a fitness coach. So don't worry. It's more about stretching out your muscles and getting your mind into alignment. After we do some poses, I'll take you to the track so we can fit in some cardio. I just wanted us to start with yoga today to mix things up a bit," he elaborated.

"Okay. I trust you," I said, sitting down on the mat opposite Mason.

"All right. First of all, we're going to lie flat on our backs," he began.

I chuckled as I moved down into the pose, copying him. "Oh, I like this one," I joked.

"Yeah, everybody does," Mason agreed. "But now I want you to close your eyes and clear your mind, all right? Pretend you've got a broom in your hands and you're sweeping all your worries and insecurities into a little pile."

"Are you serious?" I asked.

Mason nodded from his position lying on the floor. "Dead serious. I know it all seems a little New Age-y, but I promise it'll be good for you," he said. "Give it a try."

I took a slow, deep breath and closed my eyes. I did as I was told, imagining myself sweeping up a metaphorical pile of negative thoughts. Mason led me on a sort of guided meditation as we worked our way through several different simple yoga poses. He had me focus on specific muscles at a time, counting slowly to ten and back, measuring my breathing and clearing my mind. Even though I was pretty skeptical when we started out, it didn't take long for me to catch on. It really did feel oddly refreshing, like doing a hard reset in my mind. With every pose, I felt my body stretching out and opening up, like all the knots and tension in my body were being steadily ironed out, leaving no wrinkles, only a fully renewed body in its place. I even liked the way it burned in some poses, my body twisting around in ways I'd never imagined possible for a stiff, high-strung guy like me. But Mason was a great guide, taking his time to explain to me the point of each pose, giving me the rundown on which muscles were supposed to stretch out, what I should be feeling and doing. I eventually got to a point at which I could both follow his soft instructions and let my mind wander through the lush green hills of South

America at the same time. He led me through about a half hour of yoga poses before helping me up to my feet and announcing we were done.

"Wow. That was new," I remarked.

"How do you feel?" Mason asked.

I contemplated for a moment. "Good. It's different. But I feel really calm."

"Good. That's exactly what I hoped for," he replied, grinning widely. "Now come on, let's get you some cardio before I send you packin.'"

The two of us rolled up the yoga mats and went back out into the main area of the gym, walking past the rows and rows of buff, sweaty men with their glistening, bulging muscles. We went to the indoor track and stretched a little more before starting to jog. Mason jogged alongside me, distracting me from how quickly out of breath I became by chatting endlessly. He was in great shape, able to somehow maintain jogging and talking at the same time. I was grateful to his chatterbox tendencies, since I was too busy reminding myself to breathe to even try and keep up with the conversation. It was more like Mason monologuing than a real conversation, but that was fine by me.

"So, you and I went to high school together," he began conversationally. "You know I used to be on the football team?"

I nodded. He went on. "Yeah. Those were the days. Just kidding – it was a lot of fun, but I'm not one of those guys who peaked in high school." He laughed. "Or maybe I did. Who knows? Either way, I'm happy now. Life never quite works out the way you think it's going to."

"Ain't that the truth," I agreed breathlessly.

"Not to brag or anything, but I even got a scholarship for sports back in the day. Yep. I was all set to head off to some big, fancy college to play football, but then life happened, and I ended up sticking around Winchester for a while longer. Family stuff, you know. All beyond anyone's control. Sometimes life throws you a curveball, and you just have to make things work. My family needed me more than that college did. And I cared way more about taking care of my folks than playin' football," he explained.

"What happened to your family?" I asked.

"Well, we were doin' pretty okay with the finances and whatnot. My mom's always been really good with numbers, so she always handled the family taxes and all that. But then... well, you remember that big storm we got that summer?" he asked.

I nodded. "Yeah."

"Yeah. Well, it hit our house pretty hard. The flooding was pretty bad. Our whole basement was underwater. My little sisters thought it was fascinating, but obviously my parents were in a panic. There was a lot of fixin' to do on the family home, and it just got expensive, to be perfectly honest," Mason told me. "But anyway, I stuck around to earn some money and help out with the bills, and before I knew it, I was working here full-time and lovin' it. Truth be told, I don't think I would've liked goin' off to university. Maybe it sounds dumb, but I love it here in Winchester. I'm happy here. Why change?"

"That doesn't sound dumb at all," I said.

Mason smiled wistfully. "Thanks, man. Anyway, sorry for talking your ear off. You're a damn good listener I guess." He chuckled.

"It's helpful, actually," I panted. "Keeps me distracted from how sweaty I am."

We both laughed at that one, and before long, it was time to wrap up our jog. As we headed for a cool-down stretch, we got to chatting about the renovations at my grandmother's house. We talked about the crew, and as it turned out, Mason knew a couple of them.

Then again, I reminded myself, that was the thing about small towns: everybody knew everybody. And everybody knew each other's business.

CARTER

As we stepped through the sliding doors of the hardware store that afternoon, I stretched my arms out and beamed at the familiar sight. Mark walked by my side and looked up at the high ceiling and industrial, barebones aesthetic of the whole store. It was time to get the raised bed garden off the ground, and this was our first shop. And I couldn't lie, I was pretty excited to go hardware shopping with Mark.

"I can tell you're in your element," Mark said, smiling at me as I headed toward the lumber section without having to glance at the signs.

"The hardware store is your best friend," I said without missing a beat. "And in a place like Winchester, they do good business. Really good."

"I bet." Mark chuckled. "Wood has to come from somewhere."

"Fortunately, we don't have to go far," I said proudly as we rounded the corner into the lumber aisle. "What I'm after is that bin right there."

We approached the clearance section of wood, where there was a pile of various pieces of lumber, different shapes and sizes, all of them imperfect in some way. I picked up various pieces and examined them, trying to decide which ones were long enough for our purposes without being too badly damaged.

"All the things in here are cheap as dirt since they're damaged goods," I said, running my hand along a piece and gripping it to feel its hardness. "But that's a good thing for a raised bed garden. The wood's going to decay anyway, so you'll need to change it out in a few years. And that's why I'm gonna teach you how to build it right the first time," I added to him with a wink that made him blush faintly.

Once we had picked out some wood and gotten it cut the way I needed it, we headed to the garden section to pick out some vegetables and herbs. It was early enough in the year that it was a good time to sew, and I was happy to help design a garden that Miss Nancy would be proud to run, so rather than trying to decide what she'd want, we got a little of everything. If we had anything to say about it, she wouldn't have to do much grocery shopping for produce come harvest time.

We picked up a few other odds and ends, then piled the lot into my truck and headed back to Miss Nancy's place. By the time we pulled up, the work for the day was already coming to a close, since it was just after five and the crew was running behind on packing up. Before Mark was even out of the truck, I had hurried around to the bed and gotten out the wood.

"Do you want to try to do this tonight?" Mark asked, chuckling.

"We still got some light for another hour or two," I said with a grin. "That's more than enough to get started, at least. Unless you're not feeling up to it, of course. You learn to not waste a minute of daylight in my line of work."

"Of course I'm up to it," Mark said with some feigned, joking pride. "I know everything about raised bed gardens and making them. Totally know exactly what I'm doing."

"Uh-huh." I laughed, nodding for him to follow me. "Let's get to where I have in mind, and we'll put that to the test."

We made our way around the house and waved to some of the construction guys who saw us on the way out, most of them only carrying out what they absolutely couldn't leave on-site. Crickets were already chirping, but the burning disc in the sky was still over the tops of the trees, so I felt pretty good about getting started while we still had daylight to spare. Honestly, I just liked the idea of being able to teach Mark how to do something he could use to improve his life. I was still surprised that he was so interested in the hands-on way people in my line of work tackled hobbies, and I was even happier to indulge his interest.

Besides, I liked every chance I got to hang out with him, plain and simple. I didn't think of myself as a very complicated man, but I knew what I enjoyed.

"All right, I don't think I've shown you any of this yet," I said as we headed around to the backyard, "but I've got a few things planned out to make it easier on us."

Sure enough, we soon came into view of the large rectangle I had marked off with wooden pegs, and I set down the wood and reached for my toolbelt with one hand while gesturing to the whole setup with the other.

"So, what I've got here is an outline of one big rectangle," I explained, "and we're gonna build four smaller squares inside that, plus one smaller rectangle. With me so far?"

"I think so," Mark said, stroking his chin in faux thought. "Are you sure there are no triangles?"

"Absolutely no triangles," I said, grinning and playing along. "Triangles are for amateurs. And if you're even thinking about a circular garden, forget about it. But since we're self-respecting square builders, here's the plan: the four square gardens will each hold herbs and vegetables, and we're going to have different plants in each one. The center rectangle will hold just a bunch of pretty flowering plants. That's what attracts your pollinators. Sure, herbs and vegetables usually flower too, but I don't think Miss Nancy will shy away from any excuse to have some nice blooms come next spring," I added. "...what?"

Mark was fighting to keep a smile off his face, and he shook his head.

"Sorry, I'm still getting over the visual of you visiting Atlanta and shaking your fist at some triangular community garden or some-thing." He snickered.

"Hey, if you get serious about garden design, some people do *not* screw around." I chuckled.

"So, dumb question, but why different things in each garden?" he asked as I started laying out the wood.

"Crop rotation," I replied. "Some plants take too much from the soil, others add to it. So, you move your plants around to new soil every season. Joking aside, that's why four squares is a good place to start with a garden. Just move everything to the right each year."

"Huh, learn something every day," Mark mused.

"And you're about to learn how to build a square out of planks," I said, beckoning him over, "so grab a hammer and come over here."

Over the next hour or so, I walked Mark through the basics of how to build a raised bed garden. There was nothing to it, really, and if you knew what to look for, it was easy enough to come away with less than $20 for a complete garden. Mark proved both willing and eager to learn, and on top of that, he was a good student. I held his hands in place to show him how to drive a nail in the right way, and after just a few minutes of observing, I was happy to watch him hammer them in without trouble. He really seemed to enjoy watching the tangible results of his work come into shape, too.

"These beds are a little bit higher than some you'll see," I mentioned as we worked. "The idea here is to have them at about waist level, so Miss Nancy doesn't have to do much bending over. Easier on her knees."

"That's thoughtful of you. Did she ask for that?" Mark asked, tilting his head to the side.

"Nah," I shrugged off, "but I've seen her wince a little when she stands up, so I figured this would be good. We'll have a dirt walkway around the inside of the perimeter here, too."

"Does this all just come naturally to you, when you're planning things out?" Mark asked, smiling over at me with an admiration that made my heart beat faster.

I scratched the back of my head modestly. "Well, you get to know what people want after a certain amount of time."

By the time the last of the day's light was disappearing and the house lights were visibly glowing through the windows, we had completed one of the gardens entirely, and we stood back to appreciate our work.

"That was easier than I was expecting. Are you sure that's all?" Mark asked, putting his hands on his hips and smiling down at the sturdy-looking setup.

"That's the basics," I said. "And hey, don't sell yourself short, you learn quick! For a city boy," I teased, winking at him and leaning sideways into him so that our shoulders touched.

He chuckled and did the same back at me, and I was surprised to feel that his bump felt a little different than I recalled it being. I smiled and looked him up and down, quirking an eyebrow.

"Think that workout routine is already starting to show. I felt that."

"Now I know you're exaggerating," Mark said, looking down at himself. "It's only been a week, after all."

"Small changes are still changes," I pointed out, not happy to let him put himself down. "Sometimes your body wants to work with you. It just needs a push in whatever direction makes you happy."

"Well, all right, I won't argue with that." He chuckled, but as he did, his stomach growled audibly, and he rolled his eyes. "Speaking of."

"Miss Nancy is out with some of her friends tonight, I think," I said, nodding to the driveway that was still empty. "So if you're free for dinner, I think I might have an idea or two."

"Oh, yeah?" he asked. "Such as?"

* * *

ABOUT HALF AN HOUR LATER, my headlights were shining a pale light on the dirt road ahead of us that wound through the woods. A half-full moon didn't do much to help the visibility through the trees like this, but that wouldn't matter in about a minute.

"There is no way we're headed where I think we're headed," Mark said when he realized where we were.

"Hey, look." I chuckled, "I'm not the one who made South Point the nicest view of Lake Wren that there is, that was out of my hands. All I'm doing is showing my date a good time."

"Oh, this is a date now, is it?" he teased.

"Well, I've got food packed, and I'm taking you to Winchester's very own lover's lane, so I guess it is," I retorted with a smug smile that made Mark blush despite himself.

South Point was a rocky outcropping that jutted out over Lake Wren and happened to have just enough space for a few vehicles to park and enjoy a nice picnic on days or nights when the weather was good, and as good luck would have it, the spot was devoid of other people when I rounded the last bend to drive us up there.

I felt a grin of relief spread over my face when I saw that the sky had stayed clear for the ride. The stars above us shone down beautifully, and the moonlight reflecting in the still waters of the lake was downright ethereal. I turned the truck around and backed it up so that the rear end was facing the lake, and I brought it to a stop.

"Hope you don't mind," I said, "but I've always wanted to bring you out here. People can make all the 'make out point' jokes they want, but if you get past that, this view is just…" I trailed off, smiling back at the waters affectionately. "Well, come on, let me just show you."

I reached back and slid the rear window open, then climbed out of the truck along with Mark and headed to the bed, which I hopped up on immediately. Mark looked hesitant about climbing up, but I gave him a hand to help hoist him up with me. Once we were on, I went to the window and pulled out a couple of blankets I had in the back seat, spreading them out under us while Mark sat on the edge of the bed and watched me, perplexed but blushing and occasionally running his hand through his hair.

"What?" I asked at last, grinning at him over my shoulder.

"Nothing, it's just…" he said, unable to stop smiling. "This is sweet, Carter. Back in the day, I thought it would be cute to do something like this, but I never imagined I'd be doing it in my thirties. In a good way," he quickly corrected himself, and I laughed as I sat down on the blankets and patted the spot next to me.

Mark scooted closer, and as soon as he was in arm's reach, I grabbed him and pulled him down to me so suddenly that he yelped, but that melted into laughter as I planted a kiss on his cheek and hugged him from the side. We leaned against the back of the truck together and looked out over the lake, with all its shimmering beauty and the warm air of late spring all around us.

"It's a little corny," I admitted, "but I like to come out to the lake sometimes when I need alone time. And I wasn't kidding about food," I added, nodding back into the truck. "Don't tell anyone, but I made something... *vegetarian*." I said the last word as if it was controversial, and Mark laughed.

"Your secret's safe with me," he said. "It's probably a better choice than anything deep fried, that's for sure."

"They're vegetable wraps made with lettuce, tomatoes, and cucumbers from my garden," I said. "Chickpeas and beans for protein."

"I ought to revoke your Southerner card," Mark said, leaning in close to me. "Those are fighting words in most of this state."

"What can I say? I like living on the edge, sometimes." I chuckled, feeling the blush in my cheeks.

But as we sat there smiling at each other, both feeling a strange energy in us from our hunger, I felt my heartbeat change in a way that told me exactly what that tension in the air was. Mark looked gorgeous in the moonlight, and working in such close proximity to him all day had gotten me a little worked up, I had to admit.

"You're distracting on a construction site," I said in a low tone, reaching up and taking his chin in my thumb and forefinger.

"I was about to say it's hard to learn how to build from someone who's already built pretty well himself," he said.

My heart skipped a beat, and I leaned in to kiss him. My hands went to his body soon after, and before I knew it, we were all over each other in the pale moonlight. The water lapped against the banks under us as my truck rocked.

I felt his hand moving up my torso, groping the muscles that had grown so sturdy and hard over the years. My hand wandered down between his legs, and I felt his hardness against my fingers as I teased it. My thumb found the thick head, and I rubbed it through the denim of his pants. As soon as I felt that, my hands got more aggressive, and I knew what I wanted to do here.

"We're in public," Mark whispered when our lips finally parted.

"Do you not want to do it here?" I breathed back, hands slowing down.

"No, I do," he said quickly, smiling through his short breaths, "but we have to be quick."

I needed no more prompting. I reached back into the truck and dug through a bag I'd stashed back there for just this purpose, containing a small tube of lube and a few condoms. While I got that out and on, Mark cast a quick but thorough scan of the area around us before deciding that we were indeed in temporary privacy, and he undid his belt and dropped his pants.

As soon as his cock was free, I couldn't resist reaching down and giving it a few strokes with my hand. It brought me no end of delight, watching him put a hand on the side of the truck bed to hold himself up as a shudder of pleasure rippled through his body. I helped guide him as he turned around and steadied himself on the edge, bending over and giving me just enough space to do what I wanted.

I gripped his shaft in one hand as I slid my own lubed-up cock against his ass, and my bulging crown found his hole immediately. He gasped as it touched, and I stroked his cock steadily as I worked my way into him. My shaft felt hard as a rock, and the spontaneity of our actions only made me more eager. Judging by the way Mark felt in my hand, he did too.

At the same time that my cock entered Mark, I brought my lips to his neck and kissed him. He groaned as he felt me on his neck as well as in his hole, and inch by inch, I worked my way into him. His body seemed to relax and melt for me almost instantly, and within a few minutes of steady rocking and stroking, I had lodged myself deep into him to work him comfortably.

We had spent so much time on foreplay in the past that it was almost a surprise to be in him so quickly, but it gave me a new kind of freedom I hadn't yet explored. Even though we were supposed to be quick, I found time for my hands to explore his body. I wanted to feel everything he had to offer, and even though the changes were almost too small to perceive, I noticed them. I found them every bit as nice as I had before, and my hands had no shortage of material to work with as they found their way around his body. I ran them down his sides, over his thighs, and all the while, I peppered his neck with kisses and took the skin between my teeth as much as I could.

Mark arched his back for me as I fucked him, and every now and then, he turned his head, tearing his eyes away from that pristine view of the lake to look at me. Each time, I leaned forward and found his lips, kissing them as much as our positions would allow.

I felt myself getting closer, and at Mark's request, I didn't hold back. He was close too, and I could feel him in my hand, getting more taut and ready for release with each thrust. The tip of my cock massaged the innermost sanctum of his body, and the rewards of all my efforts were something I could feel in my hands. There was nothing quite like it. Being inside Mark was a fulfilling rush that I had never experienced before in my life, and I couldn't see myself tiring of it.

I couldn't hold back any longer, and my hips bucked into him like a piston. I heard the soft grunts coming from him one after another each time the crown of my cock ground against his inner depths, and I felt his balls tightening in my hand.

At last, the release took us both by near surprise, and an overwhelming burst of tension let itself unwind, starting with a white-hot burst at my shaft and unfurling its way up my body to every limb. I had forgotten that we were technically in public. I was so wrapped up in Mark that none of it mattered, and I was more than happy with that.

I slid out of him carefully, and once we had cleaned up, he flopped down onto the bed of the truck, a satisfied smile on his face as I beamed down at him.

"Think we forgot to eat," I said, winking at him.

"Yeah," he breathed, chuckling. "I suppose we did, huh?"

I knelt beside him and put a kiss on his lips, then ran a hand over the side of his face.

"Night's still young," I said. "And now you've got *two* workouts done today. I guess that merits stopping to get a bite to eat."

"Can't argue with that logic," Mark admitted.

Together, we took out the food I'd brought, got cozy, and did something I had never thought I'd have the chance to do, nor something that I had expected to happen in such a short amount of time: had a romantic night by the lake... with someone I realized I was falling for, and fast.

MARK

THE DAYS WERE FLYING BY. IT FELT LIKE JUST YESTERDAY I HAD PACKED up a suitcase and driven back down to Winchester to visit, but it had already been about two weeks. The renovations at my grandmother's house were going well, mostly because we had quite possibly the best construction crew ever assembled, with Carter heading up the team. I was continually amazed at how skilled he was, how competently he could juggle all the different simultaneous projects going on at the house. The downstairs bathroom had already been completely gutted, the old dingy tiles piled into the back of a truck and shuffled off to an antique store to be cleaned up and resold to a collector along with some of the other ancient stuff lying around the house. Grandma Nancy had recruited me to help her sort through stacks of old newspapers and magazines in the den while the other men chipped and knocked out the old countertops in the bathroom.

"Oh, my dear! Please be careful with that," my grandmother gasped, pointing to the dusty magazine in my hands. I held it up incredulously and promptly sneezed as I inhaled a noseful of dust layered up over the years.

"You mean this old thing? Grandma, it looks like you haven't even cracked the thing open since the eighties," I remarked.

"Oh, it hasn't been *that* long," she protested, handing me a box of tissues for my nose.

The two of us were sitting on the floor in the den. She had a big blanket wrapped around herself, one she had knitted years ago. She had a bit of a cold, but no matter how many times I insisted that she go lie down and take it easy, she refused to relax. In fact, I was starting to think the woman had no idea how to relax. Even though she had a full team of competent men working around the clock to get the renovations done, she was relentless in her mission to 'help' somehow. Even if that meant shivering under a knitted blanket while sifting through stacks of vintage fashion and interior design mags.

"Why do you even hold on to this stuff?" I asked her curiously.

"Well, first of all, those articles were all written by someone's son or daughter," she said with typical grandmotherly sentimentality. "It's good literature, even if it's a magazine and not a novel. Didn't you study that in college?"

"Not really," I replied, flipping through the pages of the dusty magazine. "I studied linguistics, not journalism. Oh, come on. This article is called 'Ten Ways to Hide Your Cellulite From Your Husband.' You can't possibly want to hold on to this. It's total trash."

Grandma Nancy opened her mouth to protest, then promptly shut it again and shrugged.

"Hmm. Okay, that one can go in the garbage pile, actually," she said.

"Thank god," I quipped. I tossed it into the big black trash bag across the rug.

"I swear there are some genuinely fine pieces of journalism in some of those magazines, though. You can't just lump them all together," Grandma Nancy said stubbornly.

"I have a feeling most of this advice is kind of outdated," I told her.

"Maybe so. But some articles are perennial, my dear. Look at this one, for example!" she said, holding up an interior decorating journal. "Look at that floral wallpaper. It's gorgeous. You can't tell me that wouldn't look absolutely beautiful in the bathroom still today."

"Wallpaper in a bathroom is just asking for mold," I chided softly.

"I suppose you're right about that. It's still a pretty photograph, though. Besides, what if one day you have a daughter? Wouldn't she love to have all these glossy magazines to look through when she comes to visit?" she chirped brightly.

I snorted. "Not to rain on your parade, Grandma Nancy, but I think you might be getting a little ahead of yourself. Where in the world am I going to get a daughter?"

"Why, from the stork, of course," she teased, giving me a wink.

"Right. Yes. That's where babies come from," I agreed with a chuckle.

"Exactly," she said. "Oh! And look at this one! 'Five Tips for Maintaining A Perm!' See, my future granddaughter will love this kind of thing."

"I don't think people really get perms anymore," I replied.

She looked utterly scandalized. "What? Really? Are you sure?" she said, holding a hand over her heart as though it was the most disturbing piece of information she had ever heard.

"Well, maybe in Winchester they still do," I amended my statement.

"Judging by the last Easter Sunday I spent at church, I'd say so," she quipped.

"Fair enough," I said.

"So," she said, glancing from side to side conspiratorially. "Tell me all about Carter."

I froze up, staring at her wide-eyed. "Uh, no, thank you."

"Come on! Tell me! I'm just dying to hear all about your little fling," she gushed.

"Nope. Not happening. You just informed me that babies are delivered via stork, so we are not going to discuss my... my love life," I whispered.

"So it *is* love, then?" Grandma Nancy gasped. She had a huge grin on her face.

"And that's the end of that conversation," I said firmly, even though it was taking all of my willpower not to smile. "We are at least not going to talk about it while he's on the premises."

"But he's all the way outside. In the front yard. He can't hear through the walls," she said.

"Nice try." I chuckled. "But no."

She was about to keep haranguing me about it when we were interrupted by my phone ringing. I frowned in confusion for a moment – Grandma Nancy was here in front of me, and Carter was out front, so who the hell would be calling me? But I picked it up and answered anyway.

"Hello?" I said, nestling the phone between my ear and shoulder as I continued sorting through old magazines.

"Hey, man! It's me, Hunter. What are you doing today?" greeted a familiar voice.

I smiled. It was my childhood friend who still lived and worked here in town. In fact, I knew he was working at our old high school. He had been here the first day when I showed up to dinner with my grandmother, but since then he'd been busy at work.

"Oh, hey! Uh, nothing much. Right now I'm just helping my grandmother go through some stuff around the house, but other than that I'm free. Why? What's up?" I said.

"I was just wonderin' if you might want to come by and hang out this afternoon. You know, see the old campus and whatnot," he suggested.

My heart sank a little. I hadn't been back to our old school in years. It was a place of contention for me, especially if I thought about the way those bullies used to treat me there. But Hunter sounded so excited and upbeat I knew I couldn't turn him down. Besides, it had been long enough. Surely I could handle it by now, right?

"You know what? Sure. I'll be over in a few hours. That work for you?" I replied.

"Hell yeah, man. I'll be coaching, but it's just a routine practice for the team. Nothin' major. I'll meet you by the football field," he said cheerfully.

I winced but replied, "All right. See you then," and hung up.

"What was that?" Grandma Nancy asked.

I sighed. "Just the past calling to check in on me," I murmured.

"What's that, dear?"

"Oh, nothing," I said with a hasty smile.

Luckily for me, she dropped the subject as she got distracted showing me yet another old magazine, this one filled with articles about the Internet. It was kind of amusing looking at the old journals, as they worked as a kind of time capsule, taking me back to the days before everybody had ready and easy access to the world wide web at their fingertips. Grandma Nancy and I spent the rest of the morning chatting and enjoying ourselves, just taking it easy. Every now and then, Carter would pass by the big bay window and pause to smile at me. It made my heart skip a beat every damn time.

Hours later, it was midafternoon, and I was walking out onto the football field, my whole body tingling with emotion. It had been a long, long time since I last set foot on the high school grounds, and my heart was pounding. I had parked in the visitors' lot and gone to the front office for a day pass, which was a strange experience in and of itself. Most of the middle-aged women who had worked in the office when I was a student here still worked in the same positions. They even looked pretty much the same. The school itself seemed a little smaller and less intimidating to me, but otherwise not much had changed since I went to school here.

I tried to remind myself to just breathe as I walked alongside the field, watching this year's crop of kids running laps. I squinted in the hazy sunlight, shading my eyes with my hand as I located Hunter. He was standing on the sidelines of the football field, a brown clipboard tucked under his arm. He had a lanyard and whistle hanging around his neck, and he was wearing a worn-out high school T-shirt with our mascot on it. Apart from being a little thicker around the middle, Hunter looked pretty much the same as he had in school. In a way, I found that comforting. It was cool to see that the march of time had barely touched him, much like the majority of Winchester and its residents. It felt as though no time had passed by at all, and yet everything was different. I was different. Because as I looked out over the field and watched the sixteen- and seventeen-year-old boys sprinting up and down and running drills, I realized how young and innocent they all looked. How harmless they seemed. It was odd; back in the day, when I was their age, the football players had all looked so huge and intimidating. Many of them were the guys who had bullied and looked down on me, making me feel small and immature and weak by comparison. But I could see now that the bullies of my time were still just kids. Just dumb, hormonal idiots running on pure adrenaline, with no idea how the world really worked outside of the claustrophobic microcosm of high school popularity politics. They weren't really big, scary monsters – they were just kids. Dumb kids. My spirits lifted as I walked up to Hunter, who gave me a big grin as I approached.

He pulled me in for a tight, brief hug – the manly sort, of course – and then clapped me on the back hard. "Hey, man! You look great! It was good catching up at your grandma's place!" he said loudly, his voice clearly hoarse from day after day of shouting instructions at the football players.

He was the current football coach, which put him in a pretty public position as far as Winchester was concerned. In a small town like this one, football reigned supreme over almost everything else. After all, there weren't a whole lot of other attractions and events in the area. In a tiny Southern town, high school football games were a big deal, and so Hunter was an important man. Still, he seemed just as humble and down-to-earth as always, which was nice to see. I had thought the same thing about him when we had dinner at my grandma's place.

"I'm great, Hunter. Just helping my grandmother with the renovations," I answered.

"Cool, cool. How's the house comin' along?" he asked.

"Awesome. The crew we've got working on it is really talented. They're all good guys," I said. "And Carter has a real vision for the place, you know. It's exciting."

"I bet Miss Nancy's gettin' a kick out of havin' all those boys around the house, huh?" He chuckled. I nodded fervently.

"Oh, yeah, she loves it. I think she likes the opportunity to cook for people and boss a bunch of men around, to be honest," I admitted.

"Fair enough. I can get behind that." He laughed. Then he paused to shout something vaguely incoherent at the football players. I took a step back.

"Sorry 'bout that. Got to keep the boys in line. We're undefeated so far this season, you know," he boasted proudly.

"Damn. That's amazing. You must run a tight ship," I said.

He nodded slowly, a look of pure pride on his face. "Yeah. I do my best. It's all them, though, really. They're a bunch of good kids this go 'round. I'm lucky to have 'em."

"And they're lucky to have you, too," I added.

He grinned, those eyes sparkling with genuine emotion. I could tell he really gave a damn about these kids. "Some of 'em have a real chance at makin' somethin' of themselves at college. I'm hopin' to get a few of the boys scholarships for athletics. Most of the kids around here just stick around Winchester after graduation, which is fine, of course. But if I can help any of 'em get into university, well, then that's what I'll do."

"It's weird," I said quietly. "I used to be so afraid of the jocks in high school. But now, looking at those kids running around, it's like... what was I so scared of?"

Hunter nodded. "Yeah, I get what you mean. But it's all about perspective, you know? When we were their age, the jocks were a bunch of big, scary guys. But now I just look at 'em and think, damn, they were probably just as insecure as we were. Right?" he said. "I mean, I've heard the way those kids talk in the locker room, and trust me, they're harmless. Just a bunch of kids with too much energy and no clue how the world really works. They'll learn soon enough, though. And I do my best to teach them respect."

"I'm sure you do a great job," I told him honestly.

"I hope so," he said, smiling wistfully.

We spent some time chatting and catching up on the years, reminiscing and commiserating about how rough high school could be for us at times. Hunter had never had it quite as bad as I did – I was the main target for bullying back in the day. But he'd gotten his fair share of awkward, uncomfortable experiences from those days, too. It was kind of nice, actually, talking about it now that we were adults. It was all behind us in the past.

By the time football practice was over and we had to part ways, I was feeling pretty damn good about myself. I had faced a secret fear of mine by coming back to our old high school, and being around the football fields was a big deal for me, too.

I was proud of how far I'd come, and my newfound confidence led me to pick up my phone and call Carter to invite him for a dinner date. Of course, I'd have to cook at his house since Grandma Nancy's kitchen was still a mess of half-built cabinets, but I was going to be the one working the stove this time. I figured it was only fair since Carter had already cooked for me a couple times. He ecstatically agreed to the date, and I left the school, heading to the local grocery store to grab ingredients for a healthy dinner. I had been researching whole foods and nutrition lately as part of my get-fit plan, so I had a recipe in mind. I was in a great mood, looking forward to spending more time with the man of my dreams, when suddenly I did a double take.

My heart skipped a beat. Then another.

Standing at the end of the aisle was a woman who looked familiar. She didn't glance my way, but I recognized her in an instant. It was one of the girls from my graduating class, a cheerleader named Heather who had always seemed to be hanging off the arm of whatever jock was bullying me at the time. I reacted to her presence with fear at first, almost as though it was an instinct for me to see her and panic because of what had happened all those years ago. But when she didn't look at me, I forced myself to relax. After all, lots of time had passed. I was having a great day. It didn't matter if someone from my past just happened to be shopping here at the same time as me. Winchester was a small town. I'd have to deal with that. So I moved on. In fact, I was so pleased with myself for getting past it that I decided to reward myself. I decided to grab a pint of mint chocolate chip ice cream, a favorite of mine.

I was walking to the checkout line, already excitedly thinking about my date with Carter, when I heard a voice that stopped me in my tracks. Next to me in the other checkout line was Heather, with a cart full of groceries and a tall, broad-shouldered guy standing beside her.

It was Jarrod Holmsted, the guy who had been responsible for probably ninety percent of my bad days in high school. Of course he had ended up with Heather, of all people. And of course they had to be next to me at the grocery store. Still, I tried to force myself to ignore them. I stared straight ahead, not daring to look their way. And yet, that didn't protect me from *hearing* them.

"Oh my god, you're right. It *is* him," Heather hissed. "Has he lost weight?"

"Pfft. I guess so. But look in his cart," Jarrod muttered back to her.

"What? What is it?"

I could feel my heart sinking. No. This could not be happening.

"He's got a pint of ice cream in there. I bet he's gonna eat it all in one sitting, too." Jarrod chortled. "Guess some things never change, huh?"

I was frozen in place. My blood ran cold. The couple moved up in line, and I was left standing there totally paralyzed, all my hard-won self-confidence draining away. I thought I had come so far, but maybe I was wrong. Maybe all those positive changes were just in my head.

I was still the same chubby loser I was back in high school.

I was never going to be in shape. I was never going to be fast and strong and in control. I was never going to wander along the misty, mystical mountains of South America. Without the proper athleti-cism, that was a death sentence for a guy like me.

And that meant that I sure as hell didn't deserve a guy like Carter.

CARTER

By the time I finished the last of the dishes, the only thing that could have put me in an even better mood than I was already in was Mark coming over tonight.

My favorite music was playing from my laptop in the kitchen as I rolled right into sweeping the house, and I softly sang along to the slow, peaceful tune of an acoustic guitar that floated through the house. I was pretty damn picky when it came to my choice of country music, and I figured my tastes were more what you would call blue-grass than the kind of mournful country that was usually played on the radio. But I wasn't about to judge anyone's tastes, all I knew was that in the privacy of my home, I could rock out to mine and not feel a lick of shame.

And so, the moment I had arrived home after a long day, I decided I had earned a little self-indulgence. I poured myself a bourbon, hit the music and started tidying up for the date with Mark tonight.

There wasn't a soul in Winchester who could say I'd had an easy day. It had started at the crack of dawn when I had to go to the Sullivan house to check in with the construction team. The porch was finally starting to look like a proper porch, and there was just enough of it finished for Miss Nancy to sit in a rocking chair in the morning sun, enjoying a tall glass of sweet tea while the guys worked around the house.

The interior was shaping up nicely, too. I was willing to stake my license on the fact that the stairs were now in better shape than they had been when Miss Nancy first moved into the place, and the rooms that had been nothing but rubble not that long ago were now starting to look like shadows of their finished states at long last. I had to check in on everyone and make sure we were still on schedule, but we all knew we were ahead of it. That was rare, and it alone could have put me in a good mood for the rest of the day.

I couldn't keep myself from jumping in to get my hands on the physical labor with one of the guys working on the kitchen, so I was sweaty by the time I left the Sullivan house. Before heading home, I'd had one more stop to make.

I had to check in on the secret project I was chipping away at.

Calling it a secret was probably overly dramatic, but I couldn't think of a better term for it. It was only a secret to anyone who hadn't walked by it, but it was just far enough into the woods that I couldn't imagine that happening very often. My intention had been to keep it nice and private, and I was handling as much of the work on it as I could manage on my own. For everything else, and of course there were things I wasn't qualified to handle, I reached out to contacts I knew would keep quiet about the project, nobody but the most trustworthy workers in the area. As expected, my buddy's work seemed to be in order, and that meant my secret project was technically serviceable. I still had a few more finishing touches to put on it, but it was coming together wonderfully.

I couldn't wait to show Mark.

Frankly, it had been a struggle to hold myself back from spoiling the surprise and showing him before it was finished, but I wanted to show him something he might be truly impressed by. If he could hold himself back from indulging in Miss Nancy's proud Southern cooking, I could hold in a secret just another week or so. Besides, my plans for it had changed slightly ever since we had been spending so much time together, and that made this whole thing even more exciting.

Once I finished sweeping, I jetted around the house for a final pass, making sure everything was exactly the way I wanted it. I had picked up a few pine-scented candles that I lit to get the aroma wafting through the house early. I triple-checked the living room to make sure the big, heavy couch was tidy and inviting, and of course, I had a bottle of red wine and a couple of glasses sitting on the nightstand of an immaculately made bed. I wasn't sure where we were going to enjoy that wine and each other, but wherever in the house it was, I was damn sure going to be ready for it.

Finally, I decided I was satisfied enough to call the house cleaning finished. On the menu tonight were fish tacos, with fish caught fresh from the lake and most of the other ingredients grown in my backyard. I couldn't claim credit for the tortillas, so I had to take it on good faith that whoever had grown the wheat and ground it into flour had done so with love. They were sure going to be appreciated with love, if nothing else. Mark had mentioned something about stopping by the grocery store to pick up food, but I had other plans. I wanted to surprise him, so I sent him a text and told him to skip the supermarket because we were having fish tacos. The odd thing was, I hadn't heard back from him.

I got out the chopping board and prepared to cut up the vegetables and try my hand at making pico. With music filling the kitchen, I could barely hear the ping from my cell phone on the arm of the couch in the living room as it lit up with a text message. Thinking it must have been Mark checking in for tonight, I washed the onion off my hands and dried them on my jeans as I crossed the room to check it.

My heart fluttered as I saw Mark's name above the text before I even opened it. Two weeks into Mark being back in Winchester, and my flame for him certainly hadn't died down. I couldn't spend a minute in the room with the guy without feeling hot and bothered. Mark didn't seem to be getting tired of whatever it was we had going on, and that was more than good enough for me.

But after my eyes flitted over the text, I realized I had to read it again because what was on the screen was the last thing I had been expecting.

HEY, I'm really sorry for the short notice, but I need to take a rain check for tonight. Long story, but don't let that stop you from making tacos!

MY FACE FELL as I reread the text and processed what it said. It wasn't like Mark to back out of plans like that, especially without much of an explanation. I didn't doubt that he had a good reason, but it confused me that he didn't think he could let me know whatever it was. I carried the phone into the kitchen and killed the music so that I could call him, and I leaned against the counter as I listened to the ringing.

"Hey, you've reached Mark Sullivan. Leave your name and number after the tone, and I'll get back to you as soon as I can."

Beep.

I looked at the screen and screwed up my face as I heard Mark's professional voice message prompt. I called again but heard the same thing after a number of rings, even though he had definitely sent the text just a few seconds before I saw it. After a moment, I decided that he might have sent the text and walked away from the phone immediately, so I waited about five minutes before trying again.

Still nothing. I was starting to get worried, and I typed out a quick text to send him, then second-guessed myself, deleted it all, and hit *call* again. It rang and rang, and I was just about to take the phone away from my ear when I finally heard a voice that was different from the usual.

"Hey," Mark said.

Immediately, I knew something was off. His voice was muted and dull, with none of the usual spark in it that had drawn me to him in the first place. I hesitated a moment before speaking, mind racing.

"Um, hey," I said at last, rubbing my forehead and going to the window to look at the waxing moon while we spoke. "Is everything all right? I saw your text and got worried. Your car's not in trouble, is it?"

"No, no, nothing like that," Mark said, and I could almost hear him trying to come up with the next words, but instead, he said nothing.

A tense pause followed.

"Okay," I said at last, if only to break the spell. "Is it anything I can help with?"

"Uh...no, you're fine."

"Are you sure?"

"Yeah, really, it's fine."

"It doesn't sound fine," I said, finally letting more of my concern show. "Is Miss Nancy all right?"

The first thing that came to mind was that some awful emergency had come up with her, but if I was being honest with myself, I knew better than that. She was a tough woman. I figured a bear could wander into her kitchen, and the worst thing that would happen is that it would leave feeling so full that it keeled over.

"She's fine," he assured me, and I couldn't help but notice how deeply exhausted he sounded, not out of irritation with me, but it was the sound of a man who was tired of dealing with everything in general.

That wasn't the Mark Sullivan I knew.

"Anything I can do to help?" I offered, trying to sound as supportive as possible without steamrolling him.

"No, something just came up that I need to deal with," he said. "I'll catch up another time, all right?"

"Sure thing," I said, feeling my heart sink.

Mark was a lot of things, but a good liar was not one of them.

"Thanks for understanding," he said, and he hesitated before adding, "see you."

He hung up the call, and I stroked my jaw, arching my eyebrow at the phone before setting it down on the counter. This was bizarre. Mark was not the kind of guy to act like that, and it left me wondering if I had done something wrong.

I looked at the food I was about to prepare, and I decided it would be a shame to let it go to waste, but it felt just as wrong to try to enjoy it without Mark. He appreciated it in a way nobody else had, and that meant something to me.

I wondered if I had crossed a line somewhere without realizing it.

After putting the produce into the fridge for another time, I stripped my shirt off and headed toward the bathroom, planning to relax in the hot water while I thought things over. A hot shower was a good cure for a lot of things, and if nothing else, I could relax and let the tension of the day melt off me slowly.

Once I was nude, I turned on the hot water and let it cascade over my body in thin trails that ran into the drain I was peering down at. I rolled my shoulder back and ran my hands over my body, but no matter how much I tried to tell myself Mark just needed some alone time tonight, I couldn't shake my worries.

I wanted Mark to be happy, and I had been pretty sure I was doing a decent job of that so far. I didn't think of myself as any fairy-tale romantic, despite the guys at the construction site teasing me, but I didn't think I was fool enough to miss a big sign that I was doing something wrong. Had I made Mark feel objectified in some way? I liked his body at any size, and I had been careful to let him know that often without coming on too strong...or so I thought.

Maybe being in Winchester was kicking up too many memories too fast.

That thought hit me like a sack of bricks, and I put a hand on the cool tile to feel the contrast against the steaming water massaging my skin. I hadn't given much thought to the feelings Mark might have had about coming back home that weren't all warm and fuzzy. Sure, Mark himself would be the first to say he hadn't exactly had a terrible time in high school. It was hard to, in Winchester. People raised their kids right, for the most part. But there were always assholes around, and the few who had been in our lives had given Mark a hard time. That part there was no question about.

And that left me with one question on my mind: had I done enough for him to fix that?

I had never let people talk shit about other people when I was around. Even the bullies in high school had known not to run their mouths to my face, even when it was about people I barely knew at the time, like Mark. But I had never looked out for Mark, so to speak. I hadn't gone out of my way to make sure he wasn't being talked down to. At the time, I'd figured I was doing enough. I was just living my life, not any different from anyone else.

But I hadn't been as mindful of what was going on around me as I could have been. I had liked Mark back in the day, and if I had really tried, I probably could have gone out of my way to make him feel more welcome at school. Hell, we might have been able to get to know each other back then if I had only been a little more proactive.

Maybe the rush of meeting up again and starting our little romance was enough to keep that realization from setting in until now. That was certainly the case for me, at least. I leaned back against the wall and let out a breath, running my hand through my hair and looking up at the ceiling. Maybe I really had been wrong in the past. What if Mark thought I was just using him for a quick fling while he was in town? That put a bad taste in my mouth, and I hated to admit that if I were in Mark's shoes, that kind of thing might cross my mind.

And if that was what Mark thought, then that wouldn't do. I'd have to find a way to make him see that wasn't the case...and if I hadn't done enough to make him feel at home in Winchester, then that was exactly what I was going to make up for now.

And I thought I might just know how to do that.

MARK

"Sweetheart, are you feeling all right?" asked my grandmother from the other end of the long, glossy dining table.

I blinked a few times, shaking myself out of my thoughts. I had gotten caught up in my own head again, zoning out as my fork hovered halfway between my plate and my mouth. A chunk of fragrant, buttery sweet potato fell from the fork into a small pool of gravy. I stared down at it blankly. It felt as though my brain was underwater lately, my thoughts heavy and scattered at the same time. I set down my fork and looked up to meet Grandma Nancy's concerned gaze. I forced what I was sure had to be the world's least-convincing smile onto my face, and sure enough, she looked utterly unconvinced by it.

"You've barely touched your food. Are you feeling ill or something?" she asked again.

I shrugged. "No. No, I'm fine. Sorry," I said quietly.

"You don't have to apologize, dear. But I would like an explanation, if you're up to give me one," she said slyly. Damn it. She had always had a way with words, that woman.

"Explanation? Of what?" I replied, playing it casually.

But there was no hiding my feelings from my grandmother. She raised an eyebrow and fixed me with an intense, scrutinizing look.

"Come on, Mark. I know somethin' is on your mind. Let it go. Spill it," she urged me.

"Nothing is on my mind, Grandma. I'm just... I'm just tired is all," I lied.

"Now, you can't have nothin' on your mind. People are always thinking about somethin'. The day you stop thinkin' altogether is the day they lower your body into the ground, honey," she said with typical straightforward Grandma Nancy style.

"That's a little morbid, don't you think?" I said.

But she dodged my attempt to change the subject deftly. "I'm worried about you, Mark. You don't seem like yourself lately. I don't know what's changed, but I know something is wrong. You're too quiet," she said.

"I'm a quiet guy," I replied simply.

"Not this quiet," Grandma Nancy insisted softly. "And you've been hiding away."

"Hiding? I don't hide," I protested, leaning back in my chair defiantly.

She pursed her lips. "All right, then how come every time that handsome contractor is here on the premises you conveniently find a reason to disappear, hmm?" she asked.

I winced a little. Damn, she didn't miss a thing.

"Coincidence," I answered.

"Uh-huh. And when was the last time you talked to him? Face-to-face?" she pressed me.

"I don't know. A few days, I guess. It's no big deal, Grandma Nancy. Seriously, just... leave it alone, all right?" I told her.

"No can do, sweetheart," she said. "You're my grandson, and I can't just not worry about you. It's my job to be concerned, especially when you're living under my roof."

"I'm an adult. I don't need supervision, and I don't need to explain myself," I countered.

I half expected her to be offended, but I should've known better.

She was fiery but patient. Endlessly patient. Her face softened, and she lowered her voice.

"I know you don't, dear. I understand. But from one adult to another, I can't pretend like I don't see you struggling. And I may be old, but I'm not senile. I notice things. And if there's one thing I know better than anything else, it's love," Grandma Nancy explained gently.

"Love? Who said anything about that?" I murmured.

She smiled wistfully. "Mark, you don't have to say it. I can see it. And your heart is hurtin', I can tell. Maybe you don't want to open up to me about it. I can understand that. But if you won't talk to me about it, you should at least talk to the man involved. Carter needs to know what you're feelin', sweetheart, whatever it may be."

"He's better off not knowing," I mumbled sadly. "He's better off if I just let it go."

Grandma Nancy cocked her head to one side. "That seems like a decision best left up to Carter himself, don't you think? After all, he's a grown man too."

"It's easier if I make the decision for both of us."

"Is that fair to him?" she pushed me.

I bit my lip. I had a pretty good idea what the real answer was, but I said, "Sure."

"Oh, come now. You know better than that, love. You ought to give him a chance. I don't know what kinds of doubts and worries you've got bouncing around in your sweet little head right now, but you can't just tuck them away into a corner and pretend nothin' is goin' on," Grandma Nancy insisted. "Believe me when I tell you that love is never something you should take for granted. Trust me, I know better than anyone."

"What do you mean?" I asked, frowning.

She smiled softly. "I mean that love is a slippery thing, Mark. One moment it's right in front of you, shinin' and bright and beautiful, and the next moment it's slipped away right out of your hands. I've been on this planet for a long time, and let me tell you, there's nothin' more important in this world than love. You can find it everywhere if you know how to look, but that special kind of love, the kind that makes your heart flutter like a hummingbird's wings, the kind that makes you strong and weak at the same time... that doesn't come along all too often. You might not get a lot of chances to grab hold of that kind of love. So when you see it, you've got to jump on it. You've got to grab it in your hands and hold it to your chest and never let it go, no matter what, because eventually there will come a time when fate will take it away from you," she explained. I could see tears shimmering in her eyes as she spoke.

"Are you talking about Grandpa Jack?" I asked in a soft voice.

Grandma Nancy dabbed at her eye daintily with a napkin and nodded. "Yes, dear. I'm talkin' about your grandfather. He was, without a single doubt in my mind, the love of my life. The light of my world. He was everything to me. I told him so every single day of our forty-year marriage. I know you probably don't remember him very well – you were still so young when he passed. But my goodness, you would've gotten along like two peas in a pod. He was a lot like you, you know. Strong and sensitive and smart. He was good with languages, too. One year, just for fun, he taught himself Spanish. I think that's where you get it from," she mused aloud.

"Do you miss him?" I said.

One fat, glistening tear rolled down her cheeks even as she smiled. "More than anythin' in this world. Yes. I miss him. But you know what? I carry him right here in my heart. I still talk to him in my head sometimes. I tell him everything. And I still love him just as much as the day we met all those years ago. But now I don't get to see him. I don't get to touch his face and hear him call my name. He's in my heart, but he's not in this world anymore. I was lucky to have as much time with him as I did. Lots of people never find that as long as they live. So even though he's gone, I still count myself fortunate," Grandma Nancy explained with a sniffle.

"I'm sorry. That must be painful to talk about," I said.

"A little bit. But my point is... you've still got a chance, Mark. You're alive. Carter's alive. You're in the same world at the same time, and that is no coincidence. If you have feelings for this man, you need to act on them. Don't take love for granted, sweetheart. If I could have your Grandpa Jack here again, even for just a minute, I'd take it. So don't let this go without a fight, okay? Promise me you'll give it another try," she urged me.

She had a point. It was hard to argue with her on this one. I knew how wise she was, how perfectly she measured her words. She meant everything she was saying, and I knew it would be foolish of me not to take her advice seriously. But then... I couldn't help but feel like something was different. I wanted Carter, of course. More than anything. It had been a few days since I last spoke to him, as I had, in fact, been finding every possible way to avoid him whenever he was at the house working, and I missed him terribly. My heart ached to talk to him, to touch him, to be near him again. But he deserved better than me. He deserved the best version of me I could be.

"Mark?" my grandmother prompted me expectantly.

I gave her a nod. "I'll try. I promise I'll try. But you have to let me do it at my own pace, all right? I'm working on it," I told her, hoping that would be enough to placate her for the time being. To my relief, she relented.

"All right, my dear. Sorry for the lecture." She chuckled.

"No, you're right. You're always right," I teased gently. I stood up and picked up my plate to take it to the kitchen. Grandma Nancy looked perplexed.

"Where are you going?" she piped up.

"Please excuse me... I've got something I need to do," I told her.

Before she could ask another question, I strode quickly to the kitchen and rinsed off my plate before heading back up the half-finished stairs to my room. Feeling determined, like I was on an important secret mission, I changed into athletic gear, packed a gym bag, and went back downstairs. I poked my head into the dining room to say goodbye to my grandmother.

"I'm going out," I told her.

She looked totally confused. "But it's nearly eight o'clock. Where are you going?"

"The gym," I admitted. "I have some... work to do."

"Oh. Well, all right," she replied, sounding disappointed.

I could tell she was hoping I would call up Carter and finally reschedule that canceled date, but I wasn't ready to do that just yet. I wanted to, but not until I could prove to myself that I was good enough for him. And that meant hitting the gym. Hard. So I headed out to my car and used the Bluetooth setting to call up Mason on the way. The line rang a few times before he answered, sounding surprised.

"Hello? Mark?" he said.

"Mason," I replied, "you haven't clocked out yet, have you?"

"Uh, yeah, actually. I did. I'm at home now," he answered.

Shit.

"Oh. Well, is there a chance you could meet me at the gym?" I asked.

"What, like now?" he asked confusedly.

"Yeah. I need to fit in a workout," I insisted.

"I'm sorry, man. I'm already done for the day. I'm cooking dinner as we speak," he said.

"Ah. Okay," I replied, feeling crestfallen. "I guess that makes sense for the hour."

"Yeah. Sorry, Mark. I clocked out two hours ago. But I'll be back in the gym bright and early tomorrow morning if you'd like to reschedule for then?" he offered.

I considered it for a few seconds, then replied, "Oh, no, that's okay. I'll go alone. Don't worry about it. Sorry to interrupt your evening like this."

"No problem, man. But Mark, remember to be careful, okay? I know you're ambitious about your fitness, but don't push yourself too hard and burn out. You've already been working your body to the limit lately, and the last thing you need is to tear a muscle or some-thin' that'll set you back. You have to let yourself heal from the last workout," he warned me.

"Mhm. Got it. Thanks. Have a good night," I said quickly and hung up.

I knew, on some level in the back of my mind, that he was right. But all I could think about as I drove to the gym was that encounter at the grocery store, the blast from my past. I could still so clearly hear Jarrod's voice as he guffawed to his cheerleader wife about how some things never change. About how I hadn't changed. Those words stung in my mind like a poison, jabbing me no matter which way I turned to avoid it. He had somehow managed to tap into my deepest insecurity and stretch it out, making my demons taller and stronger than they were before. I had spent so many years growing up and moving past the lies those bullies had told me back in the day, and yet all it took was one offhand comment to unravel my hard work. I wanted to be good enough for Carter, but I couldn't do that the way I was now. I needed to get to the gym, work my body even harder, push past my limits. I wanted to get in shape and be the kind of man nobody could criticize. I wanted to be strong and fit and perfect. Carter deserved nothing less than perfection, and if I wanted him in my life, then perfection was my new goal.

When I got to the gym, it was mostly empty except for a few women on the ellipticals with their earbuds in. I walked past them to the back of the gym where the indoor track was located. I was determined. I was angry – at Jarrod for calling me out, at Grandma Nancy for reminding me that I was screwing things up with Carter, at Mason for not being here when I needed him, and most of all, at myself. For everything.

I was here to punish myself, to run until I collapsed if that was what it took.

So I bypassed my usual warm-up stretches and took straight to the track. I didn't even jog. I broke into a sprint as soon as my feet reached the turf. My heart was pounding, adrenaline pumping through my body like a powerful intoxicant. I let my anger, my frustrations fuel me, push me to run faster and faster. My chest was heaving, my stomach churning. It wasn't long before I felt dizzy and the room started to spin. Still, I wouldn't give up. I just kept picturing Jarrod's stupid, smarmy face next to me in the checkout line at the store. I kept hearing his dopey voice as he talked smack about me to his pretty wife.

I thought about Carter, about how handsome and kind and perfect he was, about how I would never deserve him unless I pushed myself to the brink. So I kept running, even when it became hard to breathe and that old ankle injury from years ago began to flare up. Sharp shocks of agony electrified my ankle, shooting up through my calf, my thigh, to my back. I cried out as I stumbled over my aching, weak ankle. I fell to the turf in a heap, wincing in pain as I clutched at it. The pain came in flashes of red-hot intensity, washing over me again and again. I knew I couldn't keep running. Hell, I was going to have enough trouble just getting up and limping to the showers. I sat there on the floor just stewing in pain and frustration. I was so angry, mostly at myself. All this time had passed, and yet I had still allowed a guy like Jarrod to get into my head. One little snide comment and all my hard work was moot.

Maybe I should never have come back to Winchester. I thought I had moved past all my old pain. I thought I was strong enough to be here without fear. But maybe I was wrong. Maybe this small town would always be a place of contention for me. Maybe coming home wasn't the full-circle answer I'd been hoping for – maybe it just pushed me backward. I wasn't getting better; I was just falling behind. At this rate, I was never going to be good enough to deserve a guy like Carter. I should have stayed in the city. I should have never come back here. My past wasn't a docile creature I could visit with impunity, it still had teeth, and it was hungry for a bite of my confidence just like it always was.

So why try to keep fighting?

CARTER

WHEN I CRACKED MY EYES OPEN THAT MORNING, MY FIRST THOUGHT was that this was the worst sleep I had gotten all month. That was in large part because I didn't sleep much in the first place. My stomach had been in knots when I went to bed. I had to get up over and over again that night between tossing and turning, and when I thought that was bad enough, a dog barking in the distance paired with an unusually warm night made me get up to open and close the window repeatedly until my body finally gave out around four or so.

The simple fact was that I couldn't clear my head and relax when there was something hanging over me like this, and trying to put it off and give Mark space was not helping. I had a full, pretty rich life, all things considered, but leaving any aspect of it up to chance felt wrong and stale.

It had been almost another week since he canceled that date, and I hadn't really gotten a chance to see Mark since. I knew I was an energetic, passionate guy, so aside from my initial fears, I worried that I was coming on too strong. The first night after Mark canceled our date hadn't been too bad, because it hadn't had time to set in yet. But from the next day onward, I felt that sinking feeling in my gut that I couldn't shake. It was that persistent anxiety that I had something to take care of, but that for whatever reason, I couldn't sit down and get out of the way.

I was in limbo, and I couldn't figure out what the right way forward was.

But I did my damnedest to shake that bad feeling off. I was not the kind of guy who spent days moping around the house over anything...even something that was quickly becoming very important to me. I was an upbeat guy. People knew that about me, and they liked it, I figured. I had never gotten any complaints about being who I was. If I let this get me down, everything else would come crumbling down around me, and I couldn't let that happen. That was especially important now that we were putting the finishing touches on the renovations for Miss Nancy.

Romantic troubles or not, I wasn't going to let a client down.

But I wasn't totally out of cards, either. In fact, I had one more trick up my sleeve that I had to keep reminding myself of: the project I had ready out in the woods. I couldn't believe I had managed to pull it all together despite everything, but frankly, it had been a welcome distraction the past few days. The more the reality sank in that I had a problem with Mark on my hands, the more attractive it was to spend time working on my passion project.

I hauled myself out of bed and put myself through my morning routine. After a quick breakfast of homemade bread and butter with a side of bacon and a mug of coffee, I took a quick shower, pulled on my work clothes, and headed out.

I'd been told yesterday that unless a hurricane blew through at the last second, the porch was finished. All I had to do was sign off on the work after running a quick inspection, and then it could go to the next steps to being officially finished. I could barely wrap my head around how fast everything was coming together, but that was just how things worked in Winchester.

All of us manual laborers knew good people when we met them, and the simple fact was that Miss Nancy was good people. She had a way of bringing people together when she wanted to. It was like all of us were doing the work for our very own grandmothers, and we'd do the same for any other elderly resident of the town. We might not have had big city conveniences out here, but that just meant we had more room for small-town cooperation.

I couldn't deny that I had another reason for wanting to hit the Sullivan house as soon as possible this morning. There was a chance that Mark would be up and active by now, and as much as I knew I needed to be professional, I'd take any chance I could get to talk to him. I had texted him a few times over the past few days, but he was careful about avoiding me at every turn. He was so hard to read. I didn't get the sense that he wasn't interested in me anymore. I couldn't put my finger on why that was, exactly, but a vibe was a vibe, and my gut rarely led me wrong.

But all that gloom I brought with me got pushed away the moment I pulled up at the house and saw Miss Nancy chatting with the carpenter outside, a big smile on her face and a bigger mug of coffee in her hand.

"Well, there he is!" Miss Nancy called to me as I climbed out of the truck and crossed the yard, putting on a smile for her and Adam. "Get on over here, and let's get a seal of approval on this bad boy!"

"Don't think I've seen anyone half as excited about a porch as you, Miss Nancy." I chuckled as I shook Adam's hand and gave her a warm hug. "But I'll tell you what. I don't think I've worked on a porch that was half as fun to put together."

"This house needed some TLC something fierce," Adam agreed, nodding firmly. "Can't wait to see what she looks like with a fresh coat of paint on her."

"That's last of all," Miss Nancy said proudly. "It'll be such a lovely color they'll put it on a postcard, just you wait and see."

"I'll take your word for it." I laughed, nodding.

To my surprise, Miss Nancy looked at me funny for a moment, then turned to Adam with a sweet smile.

"Dear, I hate to be a bother, but could you do me a favor? I left my darn cell phone somewhere in the living room. Would you mind being a sweetheart and find it for me? I don't want to keep Carter here waiting."

Adam looked a little surprised, but just like I would, he simply bobbed his head and jabbed a thumb inside.

"Yes'm, let me go see if I can dig it out," he said, and off he went.

I raised my eyebrow after him because I could see the outline of a cell phone as plain as day in Miss Nancy's left jean pocket. But judging by the look on her face after Adam had his back to us, I got the impression that she knew that. She nodded toward the porch, and we walked the perimeter of it while I held up my clipboard and started checking out the carpentry I knew as well as Miss Nancy didn't need checking.

"So," she said, "I hope you don't mind me sending him off on a goose chase, but I wanted a word with you."

"Well, yes ma'am, is something the matter?" I asked, furrowing my brow and assuming she meant something about the renovations that she was worried about.

"Yes, there is, young man, and I think you know it," she said, frowning. "Don't think I didn't see that worry all over your face from the second you pulled up on my driveway. I might be gettin' on in years, but my eyes are as good as ever, and I've had two and a half times as long on this green earth of ours to learn how to recognize a man in pain when I see one. How are you and Mark doing?"

Her sudden insight took me by such surprise that I nearly stopped dead in my tracks, but I kept walking slowly, biting my lip and thinking for a moment. She had seen through me as if I were trans-parent, and I felt bad about that. She was my client, after all. But she had been Miss Nancy long before that, and I knew as well as she did that trying to stay focused on the job would just be ignoring the obvious.

"You got me there," I said with a chuckle, rubbing the back of my neck. "I, uh, haven't actually seen him that much in the past few days. He had to take a rain check last week, so I assumed he was busy with something here. Do you...happen to know anything?" I asked, almost hesitant to do so.

We were breaching professional conduct here, but I didn't think

Miss Nancy cared one bit about that as much as she cared about her grandson.

"He's been about as scarce as a snowball in Florida," she said with a deep sigh, shaking her head. "I was hoping you had talked to him. He's been acting awful funny the past few days, and I figured you two might have had an argument."

"Oh, no ma'am!" I said quickly, eyes widening. "Mark is…well, he's great! I can't imagine arguing with him about anything. That's why I've been so confused about how hard it's been to get a hold of him. So he hasn't talked to you about it? I mean, I don't want to make you play go-between. I just –"

"Save it, sonny." She laughed, waving a dismissive hand at me. "If all the young men and ladies in Winchester I've played matchmaker for over the years came over for dinner, I don't even know if *I* could feed 'em all. And those are just my neighbors! When it comes to my grandson, that's a whole 'nother ballgame."

"Yes ma'am." I chuckled, embarrassed.

"But if he hasn't talked to you or me," she went on, stroking her chin, "then he's all caught up in his head again about something. Figuring out the *what* is the trick."

My heart sank as I remembered what I had been thinking about that first night in the shower, and I swallowed.

"I might have a guess," I said, and she turned to raise her eyebrows at me. "From the way he always talked, he definitely loves his hometown, but I get the impression he could spread his wings proper for the first time when he left. And I know he's been self-conscious about his weight, which he shouldn't be, but it is what it is. I was worried that being back home might be catching up to him in a way that…might not be the best."

"I see," she said in a tone that was hard to read.

"I don't know," I said, rolling my shoulders back as we came to a stop near the newly finished bridge over the yard's pond, staring into the glassy water. "Sometimes I think I haven't done enough to make sure he felt like he had a place with us here, since I knew there were people that weren't doing that."

"I think I get the picture now," Miss Nancy said, crossing her arms. "Good on you for giving your past some thought. That's more than what a lot of young men like you do. But when your conscience tells you something, it's not just to make you feel like shit!"

I couldn't help but burst out laughing at the sound of Miss Nancy using language like that, but she just grinned and raised an eyebrow.

"Laugh all you want, but I mean it. Sometimes people need space, but sometimes you've got to track them down and *show* them their place at the table before they get the message. You can't change the past, but you can sure make room for a brighter future, isn't that right?"

Miss Nancy and I looked at each other for a few long and hard moments before I gave her a nod, hearing the wisdom in her words. I knew she was right, of course, and I had to act on it.

"Thank you, Miss Nancy," was all I could say, rubbing my eyes and swallowing the lump in my throat.

"You really like him, don't you, son?" she asked, putting her hands on her hips.

"Yes ma'am, I love him," I said, and I was shocked at myself that the words came from my lips that easily, as if they had been dying to get out to someone. "I'm sure about that. He deserves nothing but the best, and I don't know if that's me, but-"

"But you know what you need to do to *be* the best," she said.

"I know what he needs right now, that's for damn sure," I said, feeling my resolve as strong as ever through the distractions of my worries. "And Miss Nancy, I know Mark's parents aren't around town anymore, and I know this ain't professional to ask on the job, but...how do you feel about all this? About Mark and me, I mean?"

"My grandson has a good head on his shoulders," she said, beaming up at me. "He knows how to pick 'em, that's for sure, even if he needed to take his time to do that. Son, if you think you need my blessing, you're kidding yourself. You've had that your whole life! But that won't make a lick of difference if Mark starts pushing everyone out again."

"That's right," I agreed, giving a resolute nod. "You said he hasn't been around. Do you have any idea where he might be?"

"Left early this morning for goodness knows where. I had barely put the coffee on when he was out the door." She sighed. "You and Hunter are probably the two young men in town who know him best right now."

"Hunter," I murmured, eyes widening, and my face brightened up. "All right, Miss Nancy, I've got a plan. Let's get through this inspection, and leave the rest to me. I've got you covered. And thanks," I added, slowing down to give her a warm smile.

She smiled back up at me, and she opened her arms to bring me into a hug that was even warmer. Just like that, I felt welcomed into the Sullivan family in spirit.

But now, I had to return the favor to Mark before he did something unnecessary.

MARK

MY HANDS GRIPPED THE STEERING WHEEL TIGHTLY, MY KNUCKLES GOING white as I held on for dear life. It felt like every inch of my body was clenching, tensing for some big leap I was about to take. If my life was a dramatic movie, surely this would be the part where I drove off a cliff *Thelma and Louise*-style. But I wasn't driving to the edge of the world. I wasn't even driving out of Winchester, not quite yet. I was still within the city limits, rolling along the near-empty back roads of my childhood. It was midafternoon, the sun sinking to that spot in the sky where it would soon duck away for the evening. The sky above was a flat, emotionless gray, even as the clouds gathered ominously in a clump on the horizon before me. I could feel the tightness in the air, the pressure building like an overfilled balloon, threatening to burst at any moment, taking me along with it as collateral. My heart was thumping like crazy. I was running out of places to run to, low on places to hide. After all, this was a small town. Everybody knew everybody else, and everyone was always watching. I couldn't think of a single safe haven to go to, where nobody would notice me. I just wanted to disappear, but in a town like Winchester that was damn near impossible. That was why I had spent pretty much my entire day driving around in my car, trying to forget about the fact that the battery keeping it alive had come from Carter.

In fact, I was doing my very best not to think about Carter at all.

But because he was the very person I was trying hardest to hide from, it was a little difficult to put him out of my head. He had moved in there, it seemed, bringing along with him all the baggage and worries and insecurities I thought I had abandoned years ago. It wasn't his fault, of course. I knew that. Carter was a good man. Too good, actually.

And there was the problem. He was the best, and I was... well, maybe not the worst, but certainly not good enough for a guy like him. It was frightening, having to face up to the swell of emotions in my soul that begged me to go back to him, to get on my knees and beg him to forgive me for disappearing into the mist like some tragic anti-hero. I didn't want to hurt him. Not at all. The idea of causing him pain of any kind was so repellant to me that I had pretty much decided to just stay away from him altogether. It was easier this way. I couldn't break his heart, and he couldn't break mine. The only problem with this master plan of mine was that it was too late. My heart felt like it had already been broken. I was running away yet again, letting those old fears chase me out of the best shot at happiness that had crossed my path in a long, long time, possibly ever.

That was what scared me most. Whenever I thought about Carter, about his kind, handsome face and his ruggedly muscular body, his rough but gentle hands and his easy smile, I could see beyond him into a future that felt warm and cozy and all too real. I could so vividly envision the two of us lasting far longer than the couple of weeks I had left to stay in Winchester. I could see us becoming something so much more. And it was that vision that paralyzed me.

I hadn't come home to Winchester to fall in love, especially not with a guy from my rather painful past. I had tried so hard to leave all of that behind me. I had tried so hard to move on, to change every little aspect of myself so that when I came back here to this little town full of ghosts, both real and imaginary, I wouldn't be afraid. I was bigger than this town, or so I'd thought.

But then again, maybe that was the problem, too: I was too big. Still. Despite all my hard work to shrink down, to shape myself into the form of a guy worthy of love and lust and all those gorgeous adornments of romance. I wanted nothing more than to be good enough for once in my life. I had even lured myself into a false sense of comfort for a little while there. Between Mason's attentive guidance at the gym and the way Carter touched me as if I was made of something precious, something more valuable than money or anything else, I'd thought I might actually get there. I might actually turn into the perfect edition of Mark Sullivan, the enlightened and physically flawless one who deserved love and adventure and joy. The version of myself who could plan out a trip to another country and go on an epic journey, hopefully accompanied by someone tall, dark, and handsome.

But my baby steps toward that goal had been thwarted. Every time I closed my eyes, I could see Jarrod's smirking face – the scruffy face of his high school yearbook picture superimposed with the more modern version of him I had seen at the grocery store. I could hear his smarmy voice telling his gorgeous, perfect wife that I hadn't changed, that I was still the same loser he used to torture so many years ago. What little credit to self-confidence I had built up so quickly crumbled beneath me, leaving me feeling lower than low. And then I had pushed myself too hard and injured my stupid ankle yet again. I was so angry at myself – for everything. For dreaming of a happier reality, for letting myself get carried away on the lofty clouds of hope.

That was my biggest mistake, right? Believing that my happiness could ever exist in the town of Winchester. I had found a modicum of success and complacency in the big city. I had a damn good job. People respected my career, my ambitions. And most of all, in the city nobody looked at me twice. I could blend into any crowd and be absorbed into the collective, never picked on, never singled out. Nobody was waiting in the checkout line to make snide comments in my direction. Simply put, people left me the hell alone in the city. And maybe that was what I needed. What I deserved. To be left alone.

Because at least that way I was less likely to get my hopes up and get hurt.

And yet, I couldn't seem to force myself to get onto that highway and leave town. Hell, I had even packed my suitcase last night and tossed it into the trunk of my car this morning. I was prepared to cut my visit short and head home early. Just go back to the humdrum monotony of my city lifestyle. Sure, it could be boring. It could feel a little isolating. But at least it was familiar, and it was sterile. Nothing and nobody there could break my heart. Not like Winchester. Not like the people who still lurked around the grocery store aisles or watched me sweating as I jogged around the indoor track at the gym. People in the city didn't give a damn about me, but perhaps that was for the best. But then, I couldn't quite squash the little voice in the back of my mind that murmured, *what about love?*

"What *about* love?" I groaned aloud.

Surely it was better to feel nothing at all than to feel rejected. And wasn't that the danger of letting a guy like Carter into my life? I had spent all my years since moving away taking back the reins from the people who had hurt me in high school. I had just about decimated their power over me, and now I was this close to handing my heart over to someone else again? No. No, thank you. I couldn't go through that.

I made another loop around. I rolled the windows down partly, taking a slow, deep breath of piney, fresh mountain air. I gazed out into the dense, vibrantly green forest. The trees here grew tall and wise with the years of untouched progress. Nobody threatened them. The forest felt secure. It felt old. It had always been such a great comfort to me as a kid. Even though I had always felt like everyone was staring at me in school, singling me out from the group, I could always count on the trees to be impartial. The forest didn't care about the number that came up on the scale when I stepped onto it. The trees didn't give a damn whether I was hurt or broken or fearful or sad. They were content to simply be, and that was reassuring to me.

I pulled over onto the side of the road, unsure of what I was about to do. I put the car in park and stared out into the trees. I could hear nothing but the wind rustling through the branches, the distant, distorted echo of birds crying and singing from deep within the woods. My fingers hovered over the key in the ignition, the engine grumbling faintly while I contemplated my options. For a moment, I thought it might be nice to just wander out into the woods, even just for old times' sake. To say goodbye to the forest that had raised me before I hightailed it back to the city, back to reality.

But then I shook my head and pulled the car back onto the road. I didn't want the silence of the trees right now. I needed someone to talk to, even if just for a few minutes. It was a Hail Mary to be sure, but I wasn't quite ready to leave Winchester yet. Besides, it was a waste of gas to keep driving around aimlessly like this. I needed a destination, even a temporary one. So I drove toward Hunter's place. I knew he would be home by now, and he could usually be counted on to keep things quiet. I just wanted to talk to someone other than Grandma Nancy, who would absolutely try to convince me to stay.

So I kept driving and eventually pulled onto the dirt road that led up to Hunter's house. He still lived in the same cabin his parents used to rent out as a vacation home for tourists, and it was a little off the beaten path. There was only one street light illuminating the entire stretch of road, but luckily, I knew it by heart, even in the gathering darkness of the early evening. This time of year, the world turned to shadows by five in the evening, so daylight was wearing thin. I hoped Hunter wouldn't have company. I didn't want to interrupt anything. But to my relief, there was only one vehicle parked out front of the cabin when I pulled up. I parked my car and took a deep breath before stepping out. He came out onto the tiny front porch to greet me before I had even gotten halfway up the path. He was standing with his hands on his hips, squinting at me in the low light.

"Mark?" he said confusedly.

"Yeah. Sorry I didn't call first. Am I interrupting anything?" I asked.

"No. No, 'course not. Are you all right?" he said.

He sounded genuinely concerned, but then again, I *had* turned up out of the blue.

"I'm fine," I said at first, then shook my head and sighed. "Actually, no. I'm not fine. Can I come in for a little while? Just to… chat?"

"Yeah. Sure, man. Come on in," he said, ushering me into the cabin.

It was very cozy, warm, and quaint on the interior, and I was amused (even in my current state) to see that there were little white tea candles lit up everywhere. As he closed the door behind us, I turned to give him a questioning look.

"Are you expecting company or something?" I asked, gesturing broadly at the candles.

He shrugged. "Can't a guy like a little ambiance in his own home?" he said a little defensively.

I laughed in spite of myself.

"Fair enough," I replied, sitting down on the cushy floral sofa.

I could tell it was an antique, which raised the question in my mind: had Hunter gone to some local antique shop for his furniture? Then again, that was a fairly common occurrence here in Winchester. With the market so saturated with high-quality, hand-made woodwork and artisanal crafts, the standard for thrift shopping around here was probably substantially higher than most of the country.

"So, what brings you to my place on a random weeknight?" Hunter asked as he walked into the little kitchen area. "And what kind of tea would you like?"

"No tea," I said, then quickly changed my mind. "Actually, Earl Grey, if you've got it."

"Sure thing," Hunter replied. "But you have to answer my other question, too."

I groaned and cradled my face in my hands.

"That bad, huh?" he quipped.

I nodded. "Yeah."

"Tell me about it," he said.

I heard the click of the electric kettle, and then he came back to sit across from me in a big green armchair.

"I'm serious," he prompted me. "Tell me about it."

"I think I'm leaving town," I blurted out.

145

He looked surprised. "Really? Already? Don't you still have a couple weeks to go?"

"Yeah. Technically, the renovations aren't quite finished, and I promised my grandmother I would stay the full month, but..." I trailed off.

"But now you're going back on your promise because...?" Hunter urged.

I raked my fingers through my hair. "Because I should never have agreed to stay here so long in the first place. Because this town isn't good for me. Because I made a mistake, and now I'm hurting someone else as well as myself," I rambled with a heavy sigh.

"Uh-huh. And who are you hurting? Miss Nancy?" he asked.

"Shit, I guess I'm hurting her, too," I admitted, feeling defeated. "But I'm talking about this guy I met. You remember –"

"Carter Foster? Yeah, I remember. You two are all twitter pated with each other," he said matter-of-factly. I winced.

"Yeah. And I should never have let that happen," I said.

"Why not? If he likes you and you like him, then what's the problem, Mark?" he asked.

"Because he's amazing and kind and hot as hell, and I'm... well, I'm the same chubby nerd I was in high school, okay?" I confessed.

The kettle whistled loudly, and Hunter rushed to turn it off, pouring us each a cup of tea. He brought it back over and said, "All right, first of all, if you were a nerd in high school, then so was I. And second of all, that was a long time ago, man. You've got to let that shit go, or it'll ruin you."

"I thought I *had* let go," I murmured. "I was making progress, or so I assumed. But then I saw Jarrod and his wife at the store, and he said something rude about me, and it's just weighing on me, I guess. No pun intended."

Hunter rolled his eyes. "Jarrod? Seriously? That douchebag? You know he's miserable as hell, right? You can't listen to a word that bastard says. He's one of those guys who peaked in high school. That's why he said whatever he said. It's because you moved off to the city and made somethin' of yourself while he's just been skatin' by on his high school glory. He's jealous. And he's stupid, too. One time I got stuck in a group project with that guy, and let me tell you, he's dumb as a box of rocks," Hunter said, sipping his tea.

"Still, he was right. I thought I was making all this progress working on my fitness at the gym with Mason, but at the end of the day, it doesn't matter."

"Well, did you feel different? Better?" he prompted.

I shrugged. "Yeah. I guess."

"Then it does matter, Mark. In fact, that's all that matters. Why give a damn what Jarrod thinks of you? I think you're pretty awesome. Miss Nancy thinks the sun shines out of your ass. And clearly Carter is into you. So what's the problem?" Hunter surmised.

I was at a loss for words. I took a long sip of my tea while Hunter looked slightly smug.

"See? Exactly," he said with an air of finality. "Now, I'm going to go call Miss Nancy and let her know you're here with me so she doesn't worry."

"No! Don't," I urged him.

Hunter cocked his head to one side. "Come on, Mark. You know I can't lie to Miss Nancy. It's like lying to my own mother."

"It's not a lie. It's just an omission," I insisted.

"Uh-huh, and that's a fancy kind of lie," he said. "I make a big deal of teaching my team about respect and honesty, and I'm not going to go back on my word, all right?"

He went to get his phone, and I hopped up, leaving my tea on the coffee table.

"Wait, where you goin'?" Hunter asked as I rushed for the door.

"Sorry. I just have to go," I said quickly.

I darted out onto the porch and was halfway to my car when I saw a pair of headlights glowing on the dirt road. Someone was coming up the driveway, and when I realized it was a truck, my heart began to pound.

It was Carter. He'd found me.

CARTER

"Don't you pull off," I murmured as I clicked my seat belt off and climbed out of my truck.

Mark's car's brake lights were on, but it would be all too easy for him to drive away and be gone forever. I was half expecting to see the lights go dim as the car pulled off, but he didn't budge as I strode to the driver's seat window, looked down at him, and leaned an elbow on the top as he rolled it down and looked up at me.

"Skippin' town, huh, stranger?" I asked with a gruff smile that hopefully hid how hard my heart was pounding.

"Hey, Carter," Mark said with a face that told me I was closer to the truth than I'd hoped I was. "Uh... no, I was just... uh..."

"Well, hey, then if you're not doing anything right this second, I wanted to see if you'd take a quick ride with me. I want to show you something. We can take your car, if you like, so long as Hunter doesn't mind us leaving my truck here."

Mark opened and closed his mouth a few times as he struggled for words. I wanted to be firm here, but I didn't want to bowl the guy over, either. I peered down at him evenly, still leaning against the window with a steady gaze as he stammered.

"Yeah, sure thing," he said, too taken aback to say anything else. "Hop in?"

"Great," I said, grinning.

I hopped over the hood of the car and got into the passenger's seat. Mark pulled off slowly, casting a quick, anxious glance over at me.

"Head toward the power plant," I said, pointing eastward. "I'll show you where to turn off."

An uneasy silence fell in the car as Mark started to drive. It must have been a solid minute of uncomfortable sitting before Mark broke the spell.

"I know I've been kind of quiet the past few days," he started.

"Hey man, that's all right," I said before he could fill in the pause with more backpedaling.

Mark seemed somewhat surprised by my candidness, and it took him a moment to pick up where he left off.

"The workout routine has kept me busy." He chuckled.

"Sure, sure," I said nonchalantly.

"...are you upset?" he asked flat out, looking over at me.

"Not at all," I said. "Just keep driving. I'll show you."

"I don't want you to think it's because of you," he went on, but I shook my head firmly, not wanting to have this conversation before the right moment.

And the right moment was a ways up the road still.

"You don't have to explain a thing to me," I said calmly. "Just take a right up here. We'll talk once we're there."

"Are we going anywhere in particular, or just some unmarked place in the woods?" he asked.

"Yeah, I guess this is a little creepy when you think about it that way," I admitted, leaning back in my seat and putting my hands behind my head to look like I was relaxed as he drove. "All I ask is that you trust me. You'll like this."

Mark looked like he wanted to say more, but he decided against it. Over the next ten minutes, the car was silent except for me occasionally telling him where to turn. We were winding through some secluded part of the woods on an unpaved road that snaked back around toward the lake, and Mark's bright lights were the only thing keeping us out of the growing darkness as the sky started to fade out of its daylight colors and into what was shaping up to be a beautiful sunset.

Finally, I directed him to drive along the last stretch of road on a hill that was still blanketed in woods. The road went up the hill far enough that we were driving around it in a shrinking spiral, and Mark seemed to catch on that whatever we were going to was at the top.

"Carter, what *is* this?" he finally asked, and for the first time, I was able to point at it as we breached the thickest tree coverage and saw orange sunlight again.

"My secret project," I said, and when Mark saw it too, his jaw dropped.

Mark brought the car to a stop in front of a short driveway up to a small set of wooden stairs that led up to a wooden deck that I had built just a foot off the ground between four sturdy trees. The deck sported a nailed-down table and a few similarly rigged chairs, but the main event was just beyond it.

On the north side of the deck began a wood and rope bridge, just wide enough for two men to walk side by side. Fairy lights dangled from every inch of the bridge, and those lights wound all the way over to what was at the opposite end: a treehouse. It wasn't a tree-house in the way we built them as kids, either. It was a proper, livable cabin that I had built within the small perimeter of trees all around it, using those hearty, living trees like support beams. The east and west walls were taken up almost entirely by a series of panel windows that could be opened or closed easily, filling the cabin with light from either the sunrise or sunset. A tiny porch stuck out from the front of the cabin to connect it to the bridge, and I had filled it with as many potted plants of different kinds that I could find. The fairy lights from the bridge climbed up the outer and inner walls like tendrils, and in the dim light of the early evening, they gave the cabin an otherworldly glow that put us to silence for a few moments.

"Carter," Mark breathed, "is this...?"

"One fully serviceable treehouse made by yours truly, yes sir," I said proudly. "Come on, let's go check it out."

"You...you *built* this?!" he blurted as he got out of the car, jogging after me. "As in, with your own two hands?"

"Pretty sure that's what 'yours truly' means, yep," I said, winking at him over my shoulder.

We climbed up onto the porch, then crossed the bridge step by step. It barely creaked under our combined weight. Wood around here was just plain strong, and I leaned into that. I took out my keys and unlocked the front door, then stepped aside to let Mark inside.

He walked into what looked like a cozy studio apartment. The wood floor was covered by various rugs I had bought around town, and blackout curtains could be rolled down from the tops of the windows to provide some privacy if desired. And to shore that up, more fairy lights hung from the ceiling to keep that enchanted effect even without the sunlight. A massive bed took up most of the room, and a small doorway to the bathroom was on the left of it. Every piece of furniture was made from locally sourced wood by regional wood-workers, and the rich smell of fresh pine filled our noses as we stepped inside.

"Carter, you..." Mark said, at a near loss for words. "I...how long have you been working on this? This is incredible!"

"Started a few months before you got here," I said, jamming my thumbs through my belt loops and approaching slowly, smiling. "The original plan was to turn it into a small B&B for singles or couples. Something I'd have going on the side to keep my hands busy since taking over the business for Dad has me at a desk more than I'd like. I had been slacking off right before you showed up again, but I gotta be honest, you inspired me to pick it up again."

Mark blinked a few times, then looked over at me in confusion.

"I inspired you?" he said, sounding incredulous.

"Listen." I chuckled, approaching him and putting my hands on his shoulders. "You're hot as sin to me no matter what shape you're in, Mark, but the fact that it only took you shy of a month to change parts of your life that you weren't happy with? The fact that you decided you wanted to get healthier and you went out and *did* it? That takes willpower, and *that's* what's impressive to me, in a big way. Do you feel good about the changes?"

He looked stunned by my words, and I watched his worried face warm up to one of loving affection in a matter of seconds. It was funny how so few simple words could make all the difference in the world, but somehow, we both knew we needed these simple words from each other.

"Yeah, I do," he said at last, blushing. "And you're right. It's not about weight, and we've both known that from the start. Someone just...it's stupid, but someone said something to me at the store, and it made me think I- I don't know."

I squeezed his shoulders, then leaned in to press a kiss to his lips. He met me, and I felt that familiar shudder of warmth run through his body as he melted into me. I hadn't been lying about Mark's body. Whether it was soft give or taut hardness I felt on his body when I explored it, I adored it. It was Mark I was in love with, not a body image. When the kiss finally broke, we were both blushing messes, and I beamed at him.

"People are always gonna run their mouths, but here's something *I'm* saying that ought to make you think: I want to offer you this place."

Mark looked shocked, and his eyes fluttered.

"...you're kidding, right?" he half laughed.

"Yep, totally kidding. That's why I brought you all the way out here." I chuckled, rolling my eyes and grinning. "Hell no, man! This place is yours, if you want it. Probably won't do permanently, and I'm not asking you to decide to move back to Winchester right this second, but I want you to know that you always have a place here. Always, you hear me? I don't want anything making you think you aren't welcome here. You're one of our own, now and always. And personally, I'd like to think you're mine, too, because...because I love you, Mark," I admitted, feeling a lump threatening to work its way into my throat. "And that means I'm yours."

Before I could read that beautiful, shocked face, Mark drew me into a tight hug that pressed our faces together.

"I love you too, Carter," he whispered into my ear in that husky tone I'd adored since I first met him. "I was about to leave when you caught up with me, but goddamn it, I couldn't leave you if I tried."

"Your ass better not," I half laughed, half choked out, and I kissed that gorgeous and stubborn man on the lips one more time. This time with a ferocity that showed him how protective I would be of my man. "Because I'm not finished with you, and I don't think I ever will be."

"Me neither," he purred back as our foreheads touched.

My hands went down to his hips, and we stood there in a few golden, cathartic moments. We swayed in each other's arms, together, in the orange sunset outlining us through the windows and the fading light slowly handing the stage to the glittering fairy lights over us. And slowly, as our hands felt each other up in a slow, sensuous dance, we made our way to the bed.

We fell onto it together, hands on each other, and we found each other's lips immediately. We were half sitting at first, leaning on the elbows clumsily propping us up as we groped at one another and crawled further onto the bed while kicking off our shoes. It couldn't have been clearer that Mark had been feeling the tension as much as I had in our few days apart. That realization sent a wave of relief washing over me that was more refreshing than anything I could have dreamed of, and the sheer energy that was in Mark's hands as he explored my body dashed any lingering doubts that his affection for me had only grown in our short time together.

My cock pushed against the denim of my jeans, urging me to let it free. But it was more than just aggressive rutting that we had in mind today. We had just spilled our hearts to each other in a way I never expected to happen tonight. We were going to get to know each other and catch up on the past few days with all that entailed.

My hands found the hem of Mark's shirt before he found the buttons of mine, so I had the privilege of pulling the fabric up over his torso and tossing it aside to behold his figure. Seeing the changes in Mark's body was like seeing him in two different outfits he looked equally stunning in because I saw Mark as the kind of guy who could wear anything well. My eyes went from his chest to his stomach to the waist of his pants, a deliciously half-hidden secret just below the darkness of his waist.

But before I could reach down and open his belt, he'd started working the buttons of my flannel off. One by one, they popped apart and revealed more of the rippling muscles running down my body. Mark's gaze was so hungry and adoring that I couldn't remember a time I had felt so wanted by anyone. It wasn't a matter of confidence. I was as confident as the next guy, but it was another thing entirely for someone to look at me with that kind of pure, basic desire.

I was a country boy, not a poet, but that thought made me feel good in that moment.

That gave me pride as the fabric slid off my shoulders, exposing myself to Mark. It had barely hit the sheets before he leaned in and pressed his lips to my muscles, working his way from my neck down to my pecs, then across my abs. His hands moved down my back as he kissed me, and while his mouth teased the waist of my jeans, his hands groped my ass. He squeezed me and sent a shiver up my spine, and my cock pulsed. Mark brought his lips to the outline of my cock. I felt him press a kiss to it, and tension melted away from my shoulders and down through the rest of my muscles one by one.

He would have gone further, but I gently pushed him away, then onto his back so I could loom over him with a cocky smile. My hands went to his belt, and I opened his pants in a matter of seconds. He squirmed as I helped him out of the stifling clothing, and once he was free, he was naked before me. I drank in the sight for a few moments before realizing I couldn't resist myself. I dove in, scooping his legs under my arms and pressing a kiss to his bare cock. I wrapped my lips around as much of it as I could get, and I dragged my tongue up its length just to taste him.

"Fuck, I've missed this," I growled, with the wet tip of his cock still leaning against my lower lip, basking in my warm breath.

"You have no idea," Mark breathed.

I undid my belt and watched his head perk up to observe me stripping down before him. I let my jeans sink below my waist slowly, unsheathing my shaft from its restraints and letting him see how stiff and rigid it was for him. I stroked it before kicking my jeans off the rest of the way, and just like that, we were completely nude before each other.

"I've gotta say," Mark said as he approached me on his knees, wrapping his arms around my waist and bringing us so close that our shafts pressed against each other. "When I came home, I wasn't expecting to wind up fooling around with you on what's easily the most romantic date I've ever been on. About as much as I was expecting to say 'I love you' on the same trip."

"There's more surprises down home than you realize," I whispered into his ear, and my hands went to his ass.

I groped him, feeling how round and wonderful the feeling of that warm skin was. Every time I squeezed him, I felt his cock pulse against mine. We let ourselves gently fall to the side, feeling up one another's bodies in the simple, comfortable coziness of being naked with a man you feel like you could spend all day grinding with.

We kissed like we'd never kissed before, tongues getting to know each other more boldly than ever. We got sloppy. I drifted to the right of his face and ended up somewhere by his ear, so I nibbled the lobe while he found the nape of my neck and took that between his teeth. We electrified each other with how our bodies moved and ground cocks, and each pulse that we felt made us want to feel even more.

My hand wrapped around both our cocks between us and I slid it up and down, tips to bases, making both of our manhoods press so close together. I felt a burst of precome from my cock, and Mark chuckled softly, nipping at my neck one last time before he began to travel down toward my waiting cock with a hungry mouth.

MARK

ALL AROUND US, THE FOREST WAS COMING ALIVE. I COULD HEAR THE whisperings of insects and birds fluttering through the branches, the soft hooting of owls deep within the woods, the whistle of the breeze rustling the canopy. If I were to tilt my head at the right angle, I could look beyond the feathery glow of the fairy lights through the crown of tree branches and deep greenery to the velvety dark sky. It was littered with bright, glowing stars, as though some ancient god had scattered glitter across the night sky. The stars swept in a pattern along with the swirling puffy clouds in shades of dark lilac and gray, cornering the moon that hung like a great white lantern above us. The air was perfectly cool, with just enough of the breeze wafting through the slotted blinds of the windows to brush over our bare skin.

As I scooted down the length of the bed, my fingertips dragged along Carter's naked flesh, feeling the trail of goose bumps left in their wake. He was shivering ever so slightly, his chest heaving with deep inhales and jagged exhales. He was not nervous. He was not scared. He was simply so caught up in the moment that his body was overwhelmed with it, and the knowledge that someone like me could have such a profound effect on this gorgeous, wonderful man gave me a boost of confidence more potent than any endorphin. I lightly traced the tense muscles in his thighs, my palms flattening out to rub and massage his calves. He was clenching a little, watching me with wide eyes as I moved down between his legs. I calmed him with a delicate touch and a warm smile, reassuring him that everything was good. Carter smiled back at me, and the rosy fondness in his expression nearly made me melt.

"I can't believe you're real," I murmured, shaking my head slowly.

"Believe it," he replied softly.

"Maybe if I get a taste," I whispered.

I felt him tense up again as he watched me carefully lower my head down until the swollen head of his shaft was mere millimeters from my parted lips. I moved my hands back up his calves, over his knees, across his strong thighs, and wrapped my hands around his length. I licked my lips in anticipation, reveling in the glory of his hard cock, so massive and needy in my loose grasp.

I watched his face closely, following the moonlit outline of his high cheekbones and strong jaw. I watched his eyelids flutter and his mouth fall open as I moved my hands up and down his shaft, ever so slowly at first, just teasing him. His body would go rigid, then relax, in a beautiful pattern that accentuated the hard cut of his abdominal muscles in the glowy light. My eyes drank in every inch of his solid, powerful frame. I gazed at him with an insatiable hunger, not even wanting to blink for fear of missing a moment of his beauty.

I couldn't believe it. He was really here with me right now in this gorgeous structure out in the woods, a place he built with those labor-roughed, competent hands. I could only imagine how many long hours of extra work, both mental and physical, he'd had to put in to build a magical treehouse like this one. It blew my mind. Yet again, Carter was proving to me the power of just bypassing the usual road-blocks of fear and self-doubt and just grabbing what he wanted out of the world. He saw what he wanted, and he reached for it. No holding back. No fear. No excuses.

Nothing turned me on more. And I wanted to prove to him beyond a shadow of a doubt just how much he meant to me, how much his influence had altered me for the better, even in the short time we had spent together. I moved my hands a little faster, making sure to slide my smooth palms along his velvety soft skin with careful precision. I held on loosely enough to tease him, but tight enough to ramp up the tension building up and up ever higher inside of his core. I rolled my thumbs over the throbbing head of his cock, circling the sensitive spot until Carter was twitching and groaning. He thrust his hips upward ever so slightly to meet my every stroke as I picked up the pace bit by bit. I wanted to give him as much pleasure as possible. He had already given me so many beautiful gifts – the treehouse, his declaration of affection, his confidence in me, the hope that I might actually deserve happiness and love rather than just the same monotony I had been living through for years.

I worked his shaft up and down, biting my bottom lip as I watched the expression on his face slowly morph from peaceful to agitated as I brought him closer to the edge. But I wasn't going to let him go that easily. Oh no. I had a lot more planned in mind for this handsome angel.

Slowly, gradually, I lowered my head down to his cock. My eyes never left his face, and when he saw that I was opening my mouth to suck him off, his eyes went wide with need. I smiled to myself with pleasure as I pulled the engorged head of his cock between my lips. I flicked my tongue along the underside of his shaft and swirled it around the head, listening to the faint moans and gasps from his throat as I worked my magic on him. I slid my hands down to the root of his rod, taking more and more of his full, rigid length into my mouth. The thickness stretched my cheeks in the most satisfying way imaginable, and I couldn't help but let out a groan of appreciation, which resulted in a vibration down through Carter's pelvis. He shuddered and reached out, his fingers fumbling to tangle themselves in my hair as he pushed me down further onto his cockhead, urging me to take in every single glorious inch. I was happy to oblige. Overjoyed, in fact. I sucked him down, feeling the ache of my cheeks and the faint tickle at the back of my throat when I took him down to the hilt.

"Oh my word," Carter mumbled breathlessly. "Fuck, that feels so good."

"Mmhm," I hummed as I began to slowly bob up and down on his cock, letting my fingers work his shaft in tandem with my mouth.

He gasped and bucked his hips, jamming his cock down my throat. I coughed a little and my eyes watered, but my own cock twitched between my legs. I was so turned on by every little movement and moan that fell from his sensual lips. I groaned as I slurped down the salty beads of precome at the tip of his cock. It burned so deliciously on my tongue and down my throat – I wanted more. I wanted to give him everything. So I started moving faster, flicking my tongue along the underside again, licking and sucking with gusto.

But before I could push him all the way to climax, Carter suddenly held my face in his hands and murmured, "Stop. Not yet. Not like that. I want... I want more of you, Mark."

I leaned back and let his cock pop out of my mouth, glistening and slick with saliva mingled with precome. Carter sat up and gestured for me to come closer to him, hooking a finger and giving me a lidded gaze that only served to stoke the fire blazing in my core. I was burning for him, desperate to taste and touch him and hear him cry out my name. I crawled up the bed to him and bent to softly kiss him on the lips.

"You're so damn gorgeous," I murmured.

"So are you," he whispered. "Now, turn around. I want to taste you."

I was a little taken aback as I was used to giving much more than I received, but I could deny him nothing. I turned around and straddled over his face so that my hard, twitching cock brushed over his perfect lips. I gasped at even that delicate touch, a shudder moving its way up through my body.

I then lowered my head and sucked his cock into my mouth again from this different angle, flicking my tongue and trying not to collapse with shivery pleasure as Carter did the same to me. I felt his hot, wet mouth envelop the touchy head of my shaft, and I groaned. He hummed his appreciation, sending sharp vibrations through my body. It wasn't long before I was slightly thrusting my hips, pushing my thick shaft down his throat. We moaned and shuddered against one another, each of us reveling in the salty-sweet taste and the silky-smooth sensation of tongues against cock. He smelled so goddamn good. I wanted to breathe him in, commit every inch of his perfection to memory. Before long, I was stunned to feel him pressing a calloused fingertip at my clenched opening while he sucked my cock. I moaned and whimpered, almost shying away from him. But he used his free hand to grasp my hip, holding me in place while he massaged the tight band of muscles around my hole. I rocked against him, my cock sliding in and out of his slick mouth.

"Fuck, that's so good," I gasped breathlessly.

He circled my hole slowly, tantalizingly, sending shockwaves of exquisite pleasure through my body. It was an almost ticklish sensation, almost too much. My instinct was to pull away, but at the same time, I was helplessly addicted to his every minuscule touch and whisper. The sensation of his body underneath mine, his taut abdominals sliding along my less-tightened core, his hips rolling up to meet my mouth as I swallowed him down to the root again and again. We moved in perfect rhythm and harmony together, fitting like the final two pieces of a jigsaw puzzle we hadn't even known we were putting together. His hand let go of my hip, and I heard him reach over and fumbled around for a moment in the drawer of the nightstand. I held my breath, imagining what he could be reaching for in there. But mere seconds later, the answer became apparent.

I heard a soft squirting noise and then the cool sensation of something slick and wet being massaged into my tight hole. I groaned with immense pleasure, bucking against his fingers as Carter poked one finger, then two deep inside me. He was blowing my mind, able to suck my cock at the same time as he fingered my ass. The combination of bliss on bliss was almost too much for my body to withstand. My legs were quaking, my chest was heaving, and my breaths were coming ragged and short. Before long, I was so distracted by the immense rush of pleasure that I could no longer focus on sucking him off. I was moaning and twitching, barely able to hold myself up and straddle his gorgeous frame while he fingered my ass and brushed against that deep, delicious spot within me.

"Oh... it feels so... so fucking amazing," I choked out between gasps.

My cock slipped out of his mouth with a resounding pop, and I felt him shiver with delight. "You like that, hmm?" he growled.

God, he was hot as hell.

"I like it. Actually, I fucking love it," I purred, rolling back and forth against him.

"Get on your knees for me," he commanded.

Didn't have to tell me twice.

I scrambled to get off of him, moaning as I felt his fingers slip out of me. I moved around to face the headboard, crouching on my hands and knees. My whole body was quivering with anticipation, my muscles clenching up in preparation for whatever Carter had in store for me. Out in the woods, I could hear the muffled melodies of nocturnal songbirds, even the distant echo of howling wolves. A cool breeze prickled up goose bumps along my bare flesh, and I shuddered in the soft moonlight.

But Carter was there immediately. I glanced back over my shoulder to watch him rip open a little shiny square wrapper and take out a condom. I held my breath, shivering with desire as I watched him methodically roll the condom over the full, throbbing length of his cock. I bit my lip, feeling his hands rove down my body, scratching gently up my back, down my sides. I sighed with pleasure and then quickly sucked in a sharp breath as I felt the swollen head of his shaft press against my aching hole. My fingers tightened around the bedsheets and I gritted my teeth, groaning as he pushed inside. My muscles twitched and flexed around him while he filled my ass with his stunning length, pushing into me inch by inch until finally he was fully sheathed inside me. Carter rocked his hips ever so slightly, and I nearly collapsed with the overwhelming pulse of pleasure, his shaft knocking against my prostate so perfectly.

"Oh my god. Just like that," I murmured.

Carter grabbed me by the hips and began to slowly slide out of me almost completely, then push all the way back in. I groaned and shuddered against him, my arms quaking to hold me up. I heard him let out a deep growl of pleasure, his body taking over for his more coherent thoughts. Perfect. That was what I wanted – for him to lose control and fuck me hard. I wanted him to use my body for his ultimate pleasure.

"You're so damn tight for me," Carter murmured as he pushed deep inside of me again.

I cried out and whimpered, grasping at the sheets as he slammed into me again and again, striking my prostate with every erratic thrust. He fucked me harder and faster, his fingertips digging into the flesh of my sides. His hips snapped back and forth with abandon. He was losing control bit by bit, and I loved it. I felt him arch over my back, kissing softly along my spine as he slammed into my ass over and over again. I gasped and pushed back against him, meeting his thrusts with my own movements.

"Turn over," he hissed suddenly. "I want to see your face."

His cock slipped out of me for a few moments while I flipped over onto my back, gazing at Carter slack-jawed and wide-eyed. He grabbed my legs and pulled me down to him, hiking my knees up over his shoulders as he guided the head of his cock back to my ass. He slid inside, both of us shuddering and moaning in tandem. As he fucked my tight hole, Carter wrapped a hand around my stiff cock and began pumping it in the same rhythm. I was squirming and writhing with pleasure by now, my vision going dark before explosive fireworks went off behind my eyes as he fucked me harder and faster, both of us losing control.

"Do it. Fill me up," I murmured. "Fuck me, Carter."

"You ready to take it all?" he hissed between clenched teeth.

I nodded, feeling dizzy and breathless with overwhelming pleasure.

"Yes. God, yes. Harder," I gasped. "Give it to me. Please."

That must have been the magic word because moments later, I felt Carter's glorious body tense up and go rigid. He gasped my name desperately while his cock twitched and spurted hot spunk inside the condom. I clenched around him, his fingers working my shaft so that I came a mere half second after him. We both gasped and panted, our bodies shivering through waves of indescribable bliss. My stomach was sticky and slick with my come as Carter slid out of my tight hole and slipped off the full condom. He disappeared for a moment into the little en suite bathroom and then came back with a warm, damp towel. I lay there with my heart thumping wildly as he delicately dabbed me clean. Then Carter crawled back into bed and collapsed beside me. I snuggled up closer to him, both of us sharing the warmth of our bodies combined.

"You're one hell of a man, Mark Sullivan," he muttered fondly.

I kissed him gently on the lips. "So are you, Carter Foster."

And with that, we drifted off to sleep together, wrapped safely in each other's arms.

* * *

THE NEXT EVENING, we were all gathered around the big dining table in Grandma Nancy's newly renovated house. It was a big party involving all of the construction crew, my friends Hunter and Mason, and of course Carter and me. Truth be told, I was still in a joyful daze after the intense lovemaking I shared with Carter in the treehouse the night before, but I was doing my best to act natural. Still, Carter held my hand under the table, and every time he gave it a little squeeze, my heart skipped a beat. That man had me wrapped around his finger for sure, but I didn't mind at all. In fact, I couldn't remember a time when I had felt this happy, this complete. The dinner was a happy affair, everybody chatting and laughing and oohing and ahhing at the finished product that was my grandmother's house. Everyone was so pleased with the results, and I could tell having us all around the table for a meal was going to become one of Grandma Nancy's most-prized memories. In fact, toward the end of the meal, she insisted that we all take a group photo so she could frame it and put it over the fireplace. Of course, nobody could tell her no. I suppose in a way we were all wrapped around her finger, too.

The whole evening was a blast. Platter after platter of delicious, comforting Southern food was brought out to the table, and the wine was flowing endlessly. After dinner, Grandma Nancy somehow managed to rope us all into playing card games – all of which she won with shining colors. The evening spiraled on and on into the night until it was long past her bedtime. Finally, we all said goodnight, and I stood on the front porch alone with Carter, just marveling at how handsome he looked in the soft bluish moonlight.

"Do you want to come with me? We can spend the night wherever you want. My place, the treehouse – wherever," Carter offered, a glow of love in his eyes.

I smiled and leaned in to kiss him softly, my hand on his cheek.

"Tonight I'm going to stay here. Grandma Nancy will need help tidying up, plus she'll be excited to have me stay in the renovated house with her. But tomorrow morning…" I trailed off.

"Meet for breakfast?" he suggested brightly.

I laughed and nodded, squeezing his hand. "Yes. That's perfect."

"I'll hold you to it," Carter said.

"I hope you do," I replied.

"I love you, you know," he added just as he was walking away.

I grinned at him from my place on the porch. "I love you, too," I called after him.

He did a little fist pump as he got into his car, which made me laugh. I couldn't remember the last time I felt so good, so full of hope and optimism and love. This was the start of a new chapter, I could tell. I was finally becoming the version of myself I could love.

Because if a man like Carter Foster could love me, then why the hell couldn't I?

CARTER

THREE MONTHS AGO, AT THE DINNER TABLE AT MISS NANCY'S, IF anyone had told me that I would be spending part of that summer in the city of Buenos Aires, Argentina, I'd have laughed in his face. And in fact, I was still laughing, but I was laughing because there was just a little too much rum in my system out here on the dance floor of a club in San Telmo, watching Mark spin around in my arms with a rosy-cheeked grin on his face.

"I told you we should have taken the classes!" I laughed as Mark nearly spilled into my arms. "I can dance, but I don't know the first thing about the tango!"

"You're doing great. You're a natural lead!" Mark laughed, in far too good of a mood to mind that we basically had four left feet between the two of us. "Besides, nobody cares! This is Buenos Aires!"

I had to admit he had a point there.

I'd never given a passing thought to anything south of Florida, for most of my life, but when Mark first shared his half-secret pipe dream of making it down to Argentina to travel around and experience the culture, the excitement in his eyes had prompted me to suggest we make it a vacation trip in the near future. Mark had loved that idea, and I had decided it would be a fine way to celebrate his other big life change.

Mark was moving back down to Winchester.

He had told me about the decision before anyone else, and the look on Miss Nancy's face had been absolutely overjoyed. As for me, I had to admit that I had been pretty excited about it too. I'd thought my offer to let him move into the treehouse would be a long shot, and it had been, to some extent, but the best I had hoped for was that we would find a way to make a long-distance arrangement work between us. I would never have asked Mark to abandon the big city and come back to a small hometown. But he had made that call on his own, as long as I was willing to make good on my offer to let him stay in that treehouse studio until he found his own place in town. Unless he fell in love with it and want to stay there. A side benefit was that there was prime hiking territory all around him, and the muscles in his calves showed it.

Of course, that had been a month ago, and I was starting to think about offering Mark a place in my house with me. I would have offered it from the very start, but I didn't want him to think I was chaining him down. I was already conscious of that because he was staying in a place I built myself, but Mark had no complaints, so I was happy to let him do what he felt comfortable with.

All that felt so far off, compared to where we were this evening.

Technically, it was morning now, not evening. Argentinians, especially those living in Buenos Aires, apparently don't even get started on a weekend night until well after midnight, and it was pretty common for nightclubs to stay open until around noon the next day. I had always thought they knew how to party in Charleston, but from the second we had landed in this colossal metropolis, I realized that nothing in my neck of the woods could hold a candle to the nightlife here.

And that was fine by me. I was having a blast, but I knew that this place would give me my fill of the wild nightlife several times over. As long as Mark was here to enjoy it with me, that made this one big, long, fantastic dream.

The dance floor of this club was a sea of people, all of whom were about where we were as far as losing our inhibitions went. The club lighting was blinding and dark at the same time, and there were streamers of brightly colored cloth strung up from wall to wall at odd, skewed angles, giving the whole place an alien vibe that was brand new to me. Everything down here was brand new to me, and I loved it more than I expected.

And I had to admit, the sound of Mark ordering food and drinks for us at every stop in absolutely flawless Spanish was sexier than I had expected. He always had a confident, easygoing tone when he spoke, and that came out even more strongly in Spanish. This was clearly a vacation he had been prepared for.

Whatever dance we were doing was probably an insulting mockery of anything close to a tango, but that wasn't stopping us. Nobody around us seemed to mind, either. We were dancing like nobody was watching, and every time my hands brought Mark close to me and I tasted the tequila on his lips in the kiss while the pulsing sound of music filled our chests, I was reminded of how wonderful the relationship we'd built together was.

The song we were dancing to finally came to a close after what must have been fifteen minutes unless we had lost track of the change at some point, and by then, we had sobered up just enough to realize that we were starving.

"Come on, I saw a food stand on the way in I want to hit!" Mark said, grinning like a kid in a candy store as he tugged at my hand and urged me toward the doors of the club.

"You're talkin' my language now." I laughed, using my larger frame to lead him out of the club through the throngs of jovial people.

We burst into the cool night air and took deep breaths, grinning at each other that we had just survived being packed into a club like sardines and still had one hell of a good time. I was still getting used to stepping outside and feeling cool air this time of year. The reversed seasons of the southern hemisphere took me by surprise, no matter how much Mark had prepped me for it.

I had to admit, during all the Spanish lessons he tried to give me, I had been a little distracted getting lost in his eyes instead of trying to figure out how to pronounce words the way he did. I wasn't completely helpless in conversation, especially after having been here a few days, but Mark was definitely taking the lead as my guide down here.

Our boots splashed through the occasional puddle in the road, and the air was still fresh from the warm rain earlier today that had driven us indoors in the first place. High up above us, the European-style buildings and apartments loomed with the occasional line of laundry strung up between alleyways. The din of chatter that would give New York City a run for its money surrounded us. It was easy to see how a guy could get lost in this city for ages and never get bored.

Mark led us right up to an absolutely delicious-smelling street food stand that was serving up what looked like some kind of fried meat in some kind of baguette.

"That's *choripan*, right?" I asked, remembering a picture Mark had shown me before we flew out.

"*Si!*" Mark said, beaming proudly at me. "Chorizo stuffed in crusty bread, plus whatever the cook feels like putting in it."

"That sounds so damn good, man," I gushed, shaking my head. "I'm a little too buzzed to be poetic."

"We're on vacation," Mark said, kissing me on the cheek. "Every word out of your mouth is pure poetry. And speaking of being on vacation, 'eating healthy' takes a break as long as we're down here."

"Oh, absolutely," I agreed, scratching the small of his back.

He pushed his way to the table and ordered our food for us, and soon, we had a couple of piping hot examples of fine Argentinian street food in our hands as we staggered through the alleys and turned up outside a lovely public park.

We stood there together, on a wide sidewalk at the street corner of a major thoroughfare and the narrow side-street we had just emerged from. It was a wet but now clear night, the air was crisp and fresh, and even so, the same moon that shone over Winchester, South Carolina, was casting its pearly light over this sprawling city in South America.

I bit into my *choripan* and immediately tasted a burst of oily, salty chorizo in my mouth, paired with the crunch of the simple yet delicious bread that surrounded it.

"Oh my god," I said with a full mouth and nearly melted at the taste. "So, when are we moving down here?"

"I appreciate the enthusiasm, but we can make this at home, you know," Mark said with a wink.

It was funny. Even though we still technically lived apart, we spent so much time together that Mark and I always referred to 'home' as if it were the same place. In spirit, it certainly was, and that warmed my heart more than anything.

"Yeah, judging by how good this is, I might have to start a workout routine if I had constant access to these things," I admitted, and Mark bumped my hip with his as we laughed.

"God, I can't believe we're really here," Mark said for the tenth time on what was still an early day on this vacation. "I know I sound like a broken record, but this really is like, a bucket list kind of thing for me."

"Oh, I know," I said, wrapping my arm around him and giving him a kiss that tasted like chorizo. "It's becoming mine, too."

Mark kissed me back, and I had the privilege of pressing him against a street lamp post to show off my love for him in a way I'd never dreamed I'd get to do. When the kiss finally broke, he looked up at me with such a loving gaze that I felt like I was falling in love with him all over again. I had a lot of days like that, and I leaned into it.

"Thank you for coming down here with me," Mark said. "I can't tell you how much it means to have you here."

"Are you kiddin'?" I chuckled, pinching his ass. "I'd go on a winter vacation in Siberia with you. More reason to get cozy at night. And hey, I should be thanking *you* for getting me to branch out of my hometown every now and then. Dunno if I can call myself a world traveler, but uh, with you? I'd globetrot just about anywhere."

Mark leaned in, and we kissed again, only breaking apart to eat more of the drunk food we very badly needed right about that time of night. Our sleep schedules were going to be all kinds of messed up by the time we got home...not that we did a lot of sleeping at night.

Making love all afternoon to the sound of Argentinian rain on our hotel windows earlier today had been one of the highlights of the trip so far, and I fully intended on keeping that train rolling.

"Okay, okay, which way to that club you mentioned wanting to see?" I asked after scarfing down the last of my food.

"Uh…" Mark hesitated, looking around.

"I'll pull it up on the GPS," I said, taking my phone out and unlocking it.

But as soon as I did, I stared at the screen, narrowing my eyes to get a better look at the email notification I saw. My eyes widened, and a smile grew over my face. I flicked the email open, and I felt my heart start to pound.

"What're you smiling about?" Mark asked teasingly, craning over my shoulder to see what I was reading.

"Something to look forward to when we get back," I said, grinning at Mark and showing him the email. "Someone's putting together the Winchester high school reunion this summer!"

THE END

ALSO BY JASON COLLINS

His Submissive

Protecting the Billionaire

The Weight is Over

The Boyfriend Contract

Chasing Heat

Dom

Weight for Happiness

Straight by Day

Raising Rachel

The Warehouse

The Jewel of Colorado

Love & Lust

Forbidden

Made in the USA
Columbia, SC
02 August 2019